FOX TOOTH HEART

STORIES

JOHN McMANUS

SARABANDE BOOKS LOUISVILLE, KY

For my father, Barry McManus

FIRST EDITION

"The Ninety-Fifth Percentile" originally appeared in *Harvard Review*; "Elephant Sanctuary" in *The Literary Review*; "Gainliness" in *McSweeney's*; "Bugaboo" in *Oxford American*; "The Gnat Line" in *StorySouth*. "Blood Brothers" originally appeared in *Surreal South '11*, an anthology edited by Laura Benedict and Pinckney Benedict, published by Press 53.

Library of Congress Cataloging-in-Publication Data

McManus, John, 1977–
[Short stories. Selections]
Fox tooth heart : stories / John McManus. — First American edition.
    pages ; cm
ISBN 978-1-941411-10-0 (softcover : acid-free paper)
I. Title.
PS3563.C3862A6 2015
813'.54—dc23

                              2014047732

Exterior by Kristen Radtke.
Interior by Kirkby Gann Tittle & Kristen Radtke.
Manufactured in Canada.
This book is printed on acid-free paper.

Sarabande Books is a nonprofit literary organization.

The Kentucky Arts Council, the state arts agency, supports Sarabande Books with state tax dollars and federal funding from the National Endowment for the Arts.

Men are made of rock and thunder:
threat of storm to labor under.

Cypress woods are demon-dark:
boys are fox-teeth in your heart.

—Tennessee Williams

CONTENTS

FOX TOOTH HEART

ELEPHANT SANCTUARY

THE STORY OF THE CREATION of my elephant vampire songs begins on the December morning when I killed Aisling, heroine of our last album and my fiancée, in one Jaguar and fled Texas in another. The second car belonged to our manager, and stealing it was a snap, I just called down to the front desk. The valet even asked for my autograph. I signed the parking ticket and headed for I-35. Early in the tour my father, Ike Bright, Sr., had pretended to die in the tsunami in Japan; since then, he'd been hiding out near Texarkana. I guess he'd owed a lot of money. To hoard his address around America had made me feel more powerful than the people around me, whether or not their own fathers were alive. It'd had me singing "Barnacle" in a major scale so that our fans hopped to it instead of swaying.

I drove nonstop through Dallas, Sulphur Springs, and then northeast toward the Palmetto Flats, following signs for a wildlife refuge. Just over the Red River I came to the mailbox that said *Blackhawk*, my father's fake name.

He was snoring in a chair on the covered porch of a farmhouse, wearing a pinstripe suit as if he had arrived from a casino. "Dad, it's Ike," I said, kicking at his legs until he stirred into awareness of me.

"I read what you told *Rolling Stone*," was the first thing he said.

I'd explained that the Pacific Ocean had needed to swallow Ike Senior before I could write true songs about him. "I was pretending to mourn you."

"You done touring?"

"See the news?"

"I'm off the grid."

"I'm in some trouble."

He pointed over my shoulder, where I saw, studying me from a fenced pasture that stretched to the denuded hills, an enormous African elephant. It was about twelve times my size, with sickly pink splotches on its ears. "Meet Gracie," my father said.

She was plucking weeds with her trunk. I pictured her hollowed out, with the paparazzi and cops and Aisling's parents waiting inside. "Where are we?"

"Camp David. President doesn't want it anymore."

"Did you win this place with a Dolly Parton?"

Nodding, he poured whiskey for himself. I realized he wasn't joking.

"So it just arbitrarily sits beside an elephant."

He nodded. "This one talks to me in my head."

"How's that work, Dad?"

"Like you and me, but in my head."

"Is this a zoo?"

"Getting warmer," he said, his whiskey sparkling in the early light. It occurred to me he meant to profit off Gracie somehow.

A Dolly Parton was a nine-five combo in Texas Hold 'em, and my first bike had come from his refusing to fold one of those. I'd lost

my braces the same way, and had forgotten to say so to *Rolling Stone*.
It wasn't a good hand. With a Dolly Parton, you lost almost every
time. Maybe that's why the few he won sent him on a winner's tilt.

"You're selling Gracie to a zoo."

"Getting colder."

"Look, I'm in some shit."

"It's a sanctuary for old, abused elephants. They've been tortured and driven insane, and now they live on this farm."

I followed his eyes to where Gracie was grazing. I needed to
talk. Ask me a goddamn question, I was saying in my thoughts.

"Old-lady elephants, sixty years old. They each have a favorite fruit and a favorite song. Isn't that something?"

"Want to hear what's going on?"

"They're basically like people."

"So that's the refuge on the signs."

"They're private. The refuge is us."

"I don't follow."

"In any case, lots of bedrooms. Take whichever."

I wish you'd been in Japan, I wanted to say, which I realize
was petulant. I don't want to imply that I wasn't grieving Aisling.
But this is about my elephant songs. I did slam the door on my way
in, to protest Ike Senior's code of honor. The code held that men
didn't pry. No matter if the men were father and son, or the son
was a little boy; the boy had to commence the talking. I'd traded
Aisling for this, I thought as I lay down in a bedroom with faded
red walls and a view of the mangy meadow beyond the yard.
Never again would I make a seatbelt of my arms to hug her from
behind. She wouldn't drink days away anymore like the heroines
of the hardcore songs I wished to write, rather than the fey songs
I did write. My songs were about yearning, mostly. In them people
yearned to be places they weren't and do things they didn't or

couldn't do. The critics called the songs gauzy. One reviewer had written that our last album was "full of fuzz." Thinking about all that, I had a sort of temper tantrum in my head. Some ugly thoughts were churning in there when a voice said, What question do you want?

It hadn't spoken in words. More like it reached in and conveyed a feeling. I sat upright. Thirty hours and as many drinks since my last sleep. Until I saw Gracie out the window, eyeing me from her field, I thought I was dreaming.

"Is that you?" I said, facing her. My dad had said she spoke to him. All my life he'd been telling tall tales, but here was Gracie, staring at me, and a voice sounding in my head.

You said you wanted a question, she seemed to reply, again not in words but as a sensation that had me reliving the desire.

Not from you, I thought back.

From who, then?

From my father.

What question?

Every question.

Give an example, she said in my head, at which time I realized what Gracie was doing: tricking me into admitting my crime.

It was one thing to imagine confessing to Ike Senior. Ike Senior would be a pot calling a kettle black to criticize me. This was an innocent, tortured beast. Probably she wasn't speaking to me in my head at all. I shut my eyes and said good day to her, and awoke to find the sun low in the other side of the sky.

I appraised the situation. Aisling was still dead, I was still a fugitive murderer, and Ike Senior was still drinking on the porch. He had been joined by a leathery-skinned woman in her forties whose horsey jaw fell open when I came outside.

"Is this Junior?" she asked with fond surprise.

"James Junior, meet your future stepmom, Clara."

"I work at the sanctuary," Clara said. "Have you made the ladies' acquaintance?"

"I introduced him to Gracie this morning," my father said.

"From 1970 until last year, Gracie lived alone on a concrete slab. Her feet are ruined. They whipped her daily."

"Hurt elephants, you should die," said Ike Senior, with a righteous anger I didn't recognize. I scanned the meadow for Gracie, listening for her in my head. She didn't seem to be near.

"James Junior, James Senior may be the last good man."

"You're the one saving the ladies," my father told Clara, which was when I knew he must be conning her out of her money.

I thought of warning Clara what was coming, then spiriting Gracie away to safety. Gracie didn't deserve being stuck around my father; surely she had suffered enough. *Altruism fails to save deadbeat rocker from lockup*, read the ticker tape in my head.

"Elephants understand English," said Clara, her eyes adoringly on Ike Senior. "They're smarter than people. Complex in every way, and sweet."

"That's why they avoid me."

"You're not complex?"

"Or sweet."

"Gracie visits you."

"She's not either, maybe."

They continued this silly back-and-forth as if I couldn't hear. Ask me a goddamn question, I thought. When Aisling was alive, I'd kept a list of reasons to break up, topped by "Never asks me about the past." Even on coke she inquired only about the future. "Always the fucking future," I shouted back at her once, with a randomness that startled her. That's because my real fight was with Ike Senior. Ask a question, ask a question, I chanted now in my head. By the bottom of my first glass, he still hadn't done it. Even when Clara went in for ice, he glanced at me only to see if I laughed at his jokes.

"How do you shoot a red elephant?"

"With a gun," I guessed.

"With a red gun."

"All these elephant jokes, as if they're funny," Clara said when she returned. "I mean, the elephant falls out of the tree because it's dead?"

"And the idioms," my father said.

"It's awful. Elephants in the room and white elephants and pink elephants and a memory like an elephant."

"Elephants deserve better," said Ike Senior, surely playing her. I began dreaming up scenarios to make him feel bad. Claiming I'd been tricked into believing him drowned. Then I recalled replying to his tsunami email.

"Can I use your truck?" I said, only to see if he would ask my destination; it wasn't safe for me to be seen in public.

He handed the keys over and said, "No title in it."

"So just don't get caught? That's it?"

"No insurance card, either," he said, with that subtle grin that asked the world to join in his wonder at how droll everything was. I took the keys. He was doing what he believed I needed, and I hated him for it. What's the trouble, Ike, what have you gone and done? Cry if you need to cry. So vividly did I react to his not saying those things that Gracie, wherever she was, must have heard me in her head.

I hid the Jaguar in the barn behind the house, and taking the truck I accelerated down the highway. Before I knew it I was crossing the Red River. Not the best choice to enter Texas again, but my fans were all sniffly emo boys and stoned vegan girls who lived in cities, not the kind of people you find at a trailer bar above a river.

I parked under a neon sign blinking *Busch* and headed inside. In the dim interior a girl with bluebird shoulder tattoos was perched a few seats down from some big-hatted ranchers. "Double bourbon," I told the bartender, taking a stool beside the girl. It felt good not to be fleeing the country after all. The bartender poured my drink, passed it over to me. My skin tingled from being so close to the girl, but I didn't look at her as I mulled over my options. Hide out in Switzerland like Polanski. Live in a Third World capital. I would stand out by my skin color.

Maybe Moscow, I was thinking when the girl said, "You seem fun," in a pleasant Ozark accent.

Tilting my drink down my throat, I turned to face her. She was cute, with cheekbones that sloped down toward her chin in a svelte triangle. "I'm mentally ill," I said.

"What kind of music do you play?" This shook me. It's only my face, I told myself, or my messy hair or my hollow eyes.

"I'm a restaurant chef."

"Nearest restaurant's thirty miles."

"In Venice, California."

"Are there foods that stop you from feeling emotions?"

"Which emotion is the problem?"

"Sadness, and happiness."

"Well, I'm just the sous-chef, you know."

I was starting to enjoy myself. She gestured down toward the ranchers, three of them in overalls and Stetsons, ogling her. "Could you kick their asses?"

"What did they do to you?"

"Stare when I'm flirting with guys."

Ignorant of music, I told myself. I needed not to like any girls now. Favorite band probably Led Zeppelin; hillbilly twang. I sensed chaos in her when she squeezed my hand.

"So you'll do it?"

"What's your name?"

"Haley, you misogynist," she said, which cracked me up.

"I'm James," I said, wondering about my last name.

"Feel like a tequila, James?"

"I think I do." I bought us two shots.

"Welcome to hell," she toasted.

"Is that a warning?"

"You've seen this place."

I nodded yes, I had.

"Why else am I an alcoholic?"

"I drink a lot too," I told her, glad to hear that she was one.

"Yeah, where have you been all my life?"

I admit it, the word *depraved* rose to mind when I heard myself say, "Looking for you." I swatted it away with another shot of alcohol. I was having too good a time. We got to talking about drunk jags we'd been on. I told her about blacking out in the U-Bahn, and she told about blacking out in Denton, Texas. She said she wanted to die like Amy Winehouse. "Gram Parsons," I countered, carelessly naming a singer *Pitchfork* had compared me to. But nothing came of that.

We kissed to catcalls, scooted tables out of the way to dance. "Cheers, mofos," I called out to the ranchers as we maneuvered around to a country tune.

As I spun Haley, I heard someone say, "Twenty K per tusk."

I fell out of rhythm. "Pardon?" I said to a red-haired fellow in overalls.

"Pardon who?" he replied, as I steadied myself.

"You said twenty K per tusk."

"I was discussing my job."

"What line of work?"

"Know James, in the Shadwell place?"

"He in the ivory trade?"

"I'm only saying yes cause you'll black it out."

"I'll do no such thing," I said, wishing Aisling would yell at this man on my behalf. I turned to speak to her. Seeing Haley instead overwhelmed my brain in a sort of power surge. One of our LPs, *Lumber,* treats the subject of blackouts, mainly what you realize during them and then forget. The lyrics are pure fiction, since they chronicle times I've forgotten. We must have kept on talking. I caught little glimpses, which I still possess, like Haley whispering in the red-headed man's ear. Looking for my bandmates, I wandered away. The bar was shaped like one in Portugal, in Porto, where we'd played Primavera Sound. It seemed to me I was back there again. "Eu gostaria de uma cerveja," I said, and then it faded away and I awoke naked on a carpet rug.

Haley was asleep beside me. "Hey," I said, poking her.

She awoke, snuggled against me. "Hey, cowboy."

"I'm scared to move," I said, referring to my hangover, but it was a deeper dread, one I could have described only by playing music.

"As you should be."

"What's that mean?"

"You live in the Shadwell place."

"I don't live in Texas."

"This is Arkansas."

"Whatever it is," I said.

"Haley, who are the Shadwells? Well, James, they're teenage folk singers who murdered their parents and blamed it on slaves' ghosts."

So these Shadwells were in prison, I thought, where they fell in with some chick who conned them out of their home, got paroled, then met her match in Ike Senior.

"Maybe an elephant told them to," I said.

"No, it was years before those elephants."

I was thinking I might ask Haley if she could hear Gracie talking, but then her phone rang. She sat up and looked at the caller ID.

"My husband will kill you," she said.

A memory flickered and went dark again. Haley reached for my guitar. Lifting it like a weight, she raised her eyebrows at me.

"Must belong to the Shadwells," I said.

"Say why you're lying, and I'll sing one of my songs."

"Are you a songwriter?"

"Frank owns this house, is the funny thing."

"Who is Frank? What songs?"

"The songs I write," she said, beginning to strum. "I finished this one last week. It's called Three Days Thirty Years Ago."

In a sultry, rich contralto Haley sang about a boy who'd strolled the lavender rows with her in the South of France. He had woven lavender flowers into her hair, long ago in a place called the Luberon Valley. That was where she yearned to be, not Texas or Arkansas. The song soothed me into a lull, so that it startled me when Haley held out the guitar and said, "Now one of yours."

I took the instrument, held it awkwardly as if I didn't know what to do with it. "I'm a chef, remember?"

"My husband met your dad in prison."

"My dad?"

"Same name?"

"Who's this husband?" I asked, startled into another memory. It vanished when Haley's phone rang yet again.

This time she answered. I heard a man's dull monotone but none of his words.

"Okay," she said, gesturing toward my guitar.

I shook my head. She signaled again. I said no a third time.

"I won't be long," she told the phone then, as if my choice determined hers.

She hung up, got dressed. "Wish I could play," I said.

"Call me when you've learned how."

I followed her out to where a blue Corvette was parked by my father's truck. I didn't remember that car at all. She kissed me bye. As she drove away, I wanted to chase her down and shout the truth, so she would leave her husband and come write songs with me in another country, but I stood there watching her disappear.

I found Ike Senior asleep on a chaise longue. Clara wasn't around. Absurd to feel lonely after just two minutes. I sat down at a desk, where I came up with some lies that I put down in a letter to my bandmates. Then I burned the letter. By now I was in a sorry state. Bile was swimming in my stomach from the hangover, and I wasn't cut out for being disliked. Maybe my guitar would cheer me up. I carried it to the porch. Sitting in the bentwood rocker, I played *Barnacle*, song by song, until Gracie the elephant came shuffling up to the fence.

She didn't stop there. She waltzed right on into my head to tell me my songs were ugly.

"What?" I replied, although I'd heard her: the songs that comprised *Barnacle* were chintzy and fake. They were overwrought and shrill and tasteless, she said, using words that once again belonged to no human language. Those are just the ones she'd have used if she'd been human.

Which parts? I asked.

She didn't answer.

Gracie, say which parts.

All the parts.

Thinking we could understand each other better if I came closer, I carried my guitar downhill and sat on a log in her shade.

"Why are you here?"

I seek peace, Gracie replied in my mind.

With her trunk she lifted some grass into her mouth. "This is peaceful," I said.

It was until you arrived, she told me. You keep screaming for questions.

The last person I wanted those questions from was a feeble, abused old-woman elephant. "Hey, I'm good now. Let's talk about you."

Okay, let's, she said, still speaking in feelings rather than words.

She began to tell me about a two-bit circus that assembled in Kmart parking lots around the South. The brute Melungeon who ran it, Scoopy Bunn, had beat her daily with a prod. I'd never heard of Melungeons, so I knew Gracie was the one conveying Scoopy to me, but I hadn't brought a pen. The only way to remember was to put her story to a melody, and convert her nonwords into lyrics.

My anxiety over Aisling subsided as I sat there rhyming about the Florida midway where Gracie had longed for Lake Malawi. She spoke in hints and thoughts that became my lyrics. Playing guitar, I sang about her déjà vu and her dead brothers and the malarial swamp at the water's edge where she'd fallen in love. No wonder Clara grew maudlin, I thought, shepherding Gracie's inklings together in paired melodies. Already I could see her as the nucleus of a new song cycle. I wondered how I would record the songs. Elephants held captive in an alien land whose dullards still mourned the Civil War. Elephants who never blacked out drunk, a thought that before I knew it had me reliving the car wreck.

Suddenly the ground was trembling. I broke off from playing guitar to see that Gracie was turning from me.

"Wait, she was dead already," I said, "I didn't leave her to die," but it was too late, she was waddling away.

I climbed the hill to the porch. I felt pretty awful, but after a few shots of whiskey I told myself fuck it, and scribbled what I recalled of the new songs. *I heard you thumping for me in another country*, went the first line of a mournful number about Gracie's homeland fifty years ago. Then I thought, Five hundred years ago. Five thousand. What if you lived forever but never forgot?

I gave Gracie a depraved vampire mother who in the year 3000 BC rendered her undead. The heartbreak and terror were overwhelming. Over the millennia, she lost hope that she would ever forget. One day in the Middle Ages, her brain reached capacity. From then on, forming memories caused her pain. I plucked an ugly tune about it, shouting its words until my throat was raw.

Ike Senior came outside. "You'll shred your vocal cords," he said, sitting down next to me.

"Least of my worries," I said, baiting him to inquire about others.

"You were speaking to Gracie."

"I was sort of meditating."

"Hear of that family in Siberia, only learned yesterday about World War Two?"

"I guess you'll study their technique?"

"Well, it's harder these days. Used to be, you just crossed the state line."

"I need a new passport," I said, thinking he would be curious to hear why.

"Under the bed you slept in, there's a shoebox."

When I stood up to go fetch it, he laughed. "What's funny?"

"You are. Think we're in a spy movie?"

"Screw you," I said, but went to look anyway. I really did

need a passport. And there really was a shoebox, but it held only slide photographs from decades ago.

Holding them up to the light, I saw no Shadwell sisters, no people either, only calico cats. Dozens were sunbathing on the porch of that house where we were hiding. Thirty in one picture. I couldn't help feeling some calamity had wiped them out, or they'd fled en masse from the same energy feeding my new songs.

I lay down to write. Drinking, I puzzled out a refrain, a sort of theme. It's good Ike Senior doesn't care about me, I thought; this way I can focus. I jotted down titles. Elegy, about elephants mourning. Logic Train, about acumen. Hannibal, about vampire elephants still haunted by trauma from the Punic Wars. The lyrics came as fast as I could write them down. I'd tapped a vein, I could feel the songs surging with a voltage I'd never harnessed. The yearning was pitched not toward gauzy maudlin people but toward real people. If I could record and mix these somehow, I thought, and send the CD off in a predated package, I could die in a disaster of my own.

Night had fallen by the time I heard through the wall a familiar rhythm that I couldn't quite place. There was muffled talk, too, so I laid down my guitar and went to the kitchen. I found my father and Clara playing poker with three strangers.

"You're in time to buy in," said Ike Senior.

"James's kid," said Clara, as it struck me: they were listening to the trumpet solo of my latest single, "Empty Harbor."

"Fifty bucks, James's kid," said the beefy redhead to my father's left, who looked familiar.

My pulse at cocaine tempo, I sat down between the other two men and laid down fifty dollars. My father gave me a set of chips. The song's climax about lying drunk girls crescendoed into my vow to drown in Pacific water, and then damned if

"Denouement" didn't come on, final track of the album.

"Who put this on?" I asked.

"Mack," said Ike Senior, pointing to the bearded professor-type to my right.

"My girlfriend downloads stuff," said Mack.

"Porn," said the black guy to my left, and the redhead guffawed as if that was funny. I had met the redhead at the bar. Frank was his name. And the table had expanded—the sort of unreal detail that jars you awake from nightmares, except there was only a leaf in the table.

"Singer sounds cute," Clara said.

"Something less gay would be nice," said Ike Senior, reaching back to the dial of what I saw was a satellite radio.

My dirge about the feral child Kaspar Hauser gave way to Merle Haggard. I calmed down. Mack dealt me a pair of kings.

"Dollar," my father said.

Everyone pushed a white chip into the pot but Clara, who stood and turned the dial back to my song. "I folded so I could put this back on," she explained.

It occurred to me they would think it a tell, how my thumping heart made my shirt flutter as in a breeze, but I didn't care about my kings. Not even with a flop of king-five-four. Sirius XM won't play you twice in a row without a reason to. Newsworthiness, for instance. This is the end, I thought, placing a bet only in order to look normal. It got raised and matched until the pot held seventy-five dollars. For the turn Mack produced another five, giving me a full house. Meanwhile "Denouement" had reached its unsubtle pinnacle. I squeezed the table leg and kept matching the outrageous bets.

The river came: another five.

"All in," Ike Senior said.

"See you," I replied, pushing my chips in. The song was about to end, and with it my freedom. You didn't have to know Ike Senior well to see he would bluff his fortune away, swindle his lover, give up his son all in a day's work. But then the music stopped and no deejay said anything, and he laid down a nine-five off-suit.

"You know how a Dolly Parton works," he said, raking in his winnings.

Clara unplugged a phone from the stereo. Merle Haggard came back on.

It goes without saying that I'd been drinking all day. In my relief I drank more. I bought back in for fifty dollars. No one knows what I've been thinking, I told myself, not even Gracie. The wall had blocked her, and she wasn't real. None of this seemed real. Aisling had never been alive.

I'm rich, I can afford lawyers, I was thinking when I heard the word *ivory*, and turned to hear Mack whisper to Frank, "A million, in dollars."

"As opposed to what?" said Frank, which was when I recalled Haley referring to a husband by that name.

"Yen, retard," said Mack.

The ivory markets, I thought with alarm.

I tried to meet Clara's eyes, but somehow she wasn't at the table.

"Is there something to eat?" I said, because I needed to sober up.

"Tired of eating my friend's wife?" said Mack.

"In my home, my son eats who he wants," said Ike Senior.

"Give me a second," I told them, standing up.

"Take all the time in the world."

I walked to the refrigerator, found it empty. Behind me the men were laughing. The game had stopped; they were just sitting there scheming. I needed to figure this out. Was it for the smooth running of a con that Frank had let me borrow his wife? Protect Gracie, I thought, but I'd known her only two days. Look at the girl I'd loved for years.

Truth was, I'd have struck Gracie dead along with every elephant if it would have brought Aisling back.

It occurred to me to put this in one of my songs, specify in the liner notes that a fraction of profits would go to the sanctuary.

I went looking for my notepad. Along the way, I got lost, because I awoke in daylight with the words *1st blackout* written on my hand. First blackout, I lay thinking, awaiting the headache. This latest one might have been my seven hundredth or two thousandth, but I recalled one thing, the tusks. Frank and Mack had mentioned ivory. What I didn't recall was who Frank and Mack were or why they knew my songs. If they'd seen the Jaguar. If I'd forged any plan.

In hope of dredging up useful memories, I thought back to my first blackout, on New Year's Day, 2000.

On New Year's Eve, 1999, Ike Senior had arrived in Port Arthur after some years absent and announced he was kidnapping me. "If I've been praying for it, that's not the verb," my mother replied, so it came to pass that my namesake drove me across cypress swamps and oil fields to New Orleans where he said, "A whiskey before the end of the world?"

To shake my head no set bargaining in motion: you choose the label, you keep the change, we'll sit by the river—except my long-lost father gestured not to a river but to a steep, grassy hill that rose twice my height above our dry position. As if it took no effort to fool a twelve-year-old. As if you could do it in your sleep. So I couldn't help retorting, "That's a hill, you sorry bastard, there's no river."

Ike Senior looked older to me then than he did twelve years later on the elephant farm. He aged years before my eyes, this man I self-consciously believed had broken my heart. "I've lied a few times, but give a sorry bastard a last chance."

Chanting *fuck fuck fuck fuck* to staunch my hemorrhage of sympathy, I followed my father upslope. Let's get this chance over with, I was thinking as we crested the grassy hill to behold a sea lapping at a shore higher than the city.

"Gasp away," he said, earning several more years of my trust. Forever after, if I saw the French Quarter in photographs, my shame rose to that hundred-year floodplain where I'd apologized for hours on end. "Don't dwell on it," he kept telling me that night, which didn't reassure me until my first sip of Jim Beam. Suddenly it felt like the sun was bursting into the night to pour energy into me. It made Ike Senior happy, I saw as much, because we were feeling it together. Years later I would tell *Spin* I'd found my tribe at 11:59 that night, when a beautiful song I'd never heard beckoned from a bar and he said, "Neil Young."

Fireworks exploded above us. "Who'll be the first chick to suck my cock in the year 2000?" shouted a man in the crowd.

"Tawdry ending to the century," remarked Ike Senior, a statement around which I would build an EP a decade later. We began the new century on a terrace of the Margaritaville Café. "If this were a film," he said, "I'd take you to meet the whores."

"Huh?" I asked, as he poured bourbon into our Cokes.

"One of those flicks where the old man calls his kid 'Kid.'"

I felt a thrill at this open maw of uncharted country, but I was afraid.

"The father wants to help his son come of age, but the son starts hating him. Father shown to be a failure."

"What do you mean?"

"Don't the whores worry it's a sting?"

"Oh," I said, imagining myself drunk the next day, drunk through high school. If the whores didn't worry, it was because they were drunk.

"Has your mother said what I do?"

"You're a con man," I whispered.

"Folks can't hear you."

"You're a con man," I said a little louder, still afraid of him, trying to lock eyes with any wasted stranger.

"No one but you knows it."

"Mom knows."

"She guessed it. To you, I'm admitting it." And just like that, he drew me in. "Who else can I trust? No one, that's who else. And I'll tell you what, Junior, not an hour goes by when I don't miss you so much."

Tears sprang to his eyes. How could I have judged them to be false, when after years of absence he sat before me weeping from both eyes?

"I want to live with you," I said.

"There's stuff to learn."

"I'll learn it."

"I don't want you becoming a mark."

"Teach me," I said, and he began to. As he instructed me in spotting marks, I buzzed with pride. My vision was tilting to one side. Although I didn't know it, my brain had ceased making new memories. Did I like girls? Did I like penthouse suites and poker? Yes, yes, and yes, but before we could enjoy those things, I awoke at sunrise on the levee slope, with trash strewn around me.

My father stood over me with a brown paper bag. "Feel like a doughnut?"

I took one. I could smell bilgewater, and feel shadow memories lurking in my pounding head as I leaned to puke.

He tossed the bag down. "It's been fun," he said, "but we'd best head home."

"Yeah, I've had fun," I replied, standing up, and out of shame or stubbornness I'd been saying similar things ever since. If someone had been around to tell it to that morning after the poker game, I'd have said it again.

Licking a finger to scrub *1st blackout* off my hand, I went and found my father snoring in a trundle bed. It was a relief that he was alone. After all, what would I have said to Clara? Hide your elephants?

I would have broken her heart, I thought, wandering out into a windy, cold day. Gracie stood by the fence, eating some clover. I walked down to her.

"We need to get you out of here," I said.

What's it to you? she seemed to ask, raising her head.

"You're in a lot of danger."

So are all elephants, she said.

My dad cheats people and lies.

Maybe I cheat and lie too.

For a moment I was shaken by déjà vu. My next album's about you, I told her, at which point the tenor shifted in our exchange.

All along she had communicated without words, but now she conveyed no feelings either. She just put up a shield so my feelings would bounce back at me, like my concern that was driven only by my new songs, and my desire to cancel out bad deeds with good ones. "No, it's not like that," I said, fiddling nervously in my pockets. I felt a cell phone, not my own.

I looked in its music library. Both my albums were there.

"Listen," I said, cuing "Four-Leaf Cover," because I needed Gracie to perceive the sadness I felt about other people's pain. Ugly or no, the song will demonstrate it, I thought until a calliope horn sounded, redolent of circus sleaze.

Who was worse to an elephant: a killer of young women or a child who begged to see the circus? I skipped to the next track, "Mom." "She killed herself," I said to explain the ugliness of "Mom." Gracie was still plucking weeds. Who fucking cares? she seemed to ask, until I recalled that she'd heard me play it already, on the porch.

Then it hit me: she recalled it today because she would recall it forever.

By playing the song, I wasn't just making Gracie like me, I was stashing my catalogue in elephant memory.

I've always believed life has no value if no one will remember you in a hundred years. Until now, though, I'd been thinking only in terms of people. Now I saw that Gracie was my portal into eternity: if elephants survived, elephants would remember me. So I knew I had to level with her, if I wanted to get on top of my story.

Already I'd confessed by accident, via fleeting thoughts, so it shouldn't have been hard. I sucked in air, steeling myself. "Last week it was ninety-five in Austin," I said, delivering words at a small fraction of the traveling speed of memories. "The air was humid, sultry, maybe Africa feels that way?"

Gracie was pretending not to be bothered, but I could see her listening. "All day we drank on the rooftop deck of this shabby marina bar," I said to her. "Billy, our bassist, was afraid we'd get too plastered for the show, and Aisling told him, 'Don't be a gaywad, I'll find us cocaine.'"

Like everyone she'd ever taunted, Billy folded to her demand. That's the kind of girl she was, I explained to Gracie. We toasted and drank. In that winter heat we were matched to our time and place, said Ren, the guitarist. I agreed. We improvised a song about it and sang it with some politicians who'd driven up from Uvalde. In the distance the Austin skyline poked above the juniper like little filaments of wire. I had probably read that description in a book, but I put it in the lyrics just to show off. "You have a gift," said one of the politicians. I nodded, smiling. Hearing I had a gift was why I wrote songs. I loved for people to think of me as a genius who gambled ever more carelessly with his life. It turned me on to imagine dying young. By sound check we could barely walk. In the nick of time, though, Aisling came through as promised, and what a show: our shirts off for hours of noise and love that the crowd really felt for us, it wasn't the drug tricking us into believing it. Girls loved us, boys did too, and a few of them invited us afterward to a mansion on a cliff above the foam-green Colorado.

As meticulously as I could, I pieced through that night: Aisling disappearing, some girls leading me into a vanishing pool where we stripped and swam and made out until one said, "You two kiss," and I turned to see Billy there. Gaywad, I thought, guiding his head in with my palm. I made love to his tongue with mine. Was he weeping or only wet? He seemed to like it in any case. I help people, I thought as I hoovered up another line. The girls' skin gleamed in reflected moonlight. There was a full moon, and it had risen over foliage so Californian that I decided we were back home on the West Coast.

As I dried off, a man with faraway hillbilly eyes and a liter of gin said, "I'd like to book you for South by Southwest."

"If you'll give me some gin."

"This is filtered water."

"It says gin right there."

"Bar's on the terrace."

"Guess we'll play Coachella instead," I said, exulting at my wit. I turned to recount the scene to the girls, but the pool was empty. So I wandered into the garage to find Aisling alone in the passenger seat of a Jaguar XF.

I got in beside her. The keys were in the ignition, turned to accessories, and "Lumber" was on. I remember because she skipped over it with a jab of her finger. Why, was it a weak song? "It's weak because it's about you," I said, and so on until she called me a con artist like my no-good dad.

I couldn't help it, I turned the engine and gunned the car in reverse, sending the garage door crumpling off its runners.

We went screeching backward down a steep driveway. "Cheaper ways to jerk off, pissy-pants," Aisling said.

"I'm wet cause I was swimming with two girls."

"Same name, same acorn, same tree," she said, as I spun us around toward a far cluster of city lights.

I think she was too busy mocking me to buckle her seatbelt. My songs were plagiarized, my cock was small, I would never feel real love. Over her drivel I couldn't think which way led back to Sunset Boulevard. At a split I veered abruptly downhill. Her stomach must have fallen out, because she shut up.

"I don't think this is the way," she said.

"Depends where you're going."

"This goes nowhere."

Never would I have asked my fiancée the way to somewhere, but damned if a GPS didn't power up and advise, "Left turn, mate," in a congenial cockney accent.

"Follow directions," said Aisling with the force of a gavel strike, leaning in to push the wheel left with all her might. We went spinning off the shoulder. The car skidded across talus until the ground fell away and we were sailing into space. Ahead of us a cantilever bridge spanned a wide, moonlit river. I had never seen this section of Los Angeles. Aisling howled. Was she upset? "We're only having a wreck," I said, before we hit the water.

There was more—climbing the hill, hitching a ride on Capital of Texas Highway—but I trailed off. Two of Gracie's friends had appeared on the hilltop. The phone was playing the album's closer, "Turgenev." I imagined the other elephants were too far away to hear me croon a vow to commit Ike Senior's same crimes if it earned his respect in heaven, but Gracie heard. She studied me like her own eye in the mirror.

"Like I told you, I didn't leave her for dead," I said, feeling sort of desperate now for Gracie's forgiveness. Before she could give it or deny it, my song faded into a ring.

I answered. "James," said a woman the device named as Franklin Pierce. It took me a minute to figure out why she sounded familiar.

"Yep," I answered, meaning I was my father.

"Where are you?" Haley said.

"By the elephant fence."

"And the others?"

She believed I was Ike Senior. "They're on their way."

"James, stay inside while this happens."

"Sure, Franklin Pierce."

"Wait until it's all over."

"I'll sit playing solitaire."

"I've enjoyed getting to know you," she said, sounding on the verge of tears.

She hung up. When I called back, the phone gave a busy-circuits signal.

What Haley wanted, I realized, was for my father to stay in the house while she and Frank harvested ivory.

I'd been seeing evidence for days now: they would shoot the elephants, saw off their tusks, and sell them on the black market.

It would happen in thirty minutes, I thought, as Gracie languished in the mud, reading my mind as indifferently as ever. It struck me what a tiny fraction of her mass her tusks comprised. It was the same with oysters and pearls, men and their gold teeth.

And then it came to me: I had it backward, this elephant hated all human beings equally. We were torturers who had chained her in a cage for almost a lifetime. Most elephants were dead because people had killed them. In fifty years they would all be gone. What did Gracie care if I had killed a girl?

She was glad I'd killed a girl. It was one less human.

I'd known something was wrong with Haley from the moment I saw her, I told myself as I hurried uphill. If I'd wished to live with Haley in another country, half of me was bad like her. It was time to let that half die, and save Gracie whether she wanted it or not.

Alone on the porch, a beat pounding in my head, I scrolled through the phone contacts looking for Elephant Sanctuary. I tried Sanctuary. No luck. Clara wasn't listed either. I hit redial and got another busy-circuits signal. I paused for a drink. Pouring, I spotted a copy of the *New York Times* lying open to a picture of me, Ike Bright, Jr., in tuxedo and boutonnière.

In the picture I had fallen over backward in the sand in a beach chair. Beside me, Aisling, in a bikini and ball cap, was tying my shoelaces together.

I stared down at the caption until I could read a single word, *gold*. Then immediately I flung the paper out of sight so fast that a number of possibilities remained.

The lead investigator in my case was named Gold. My bounty was to be paid to Aisling's father in gold. In the wake of my new notoriety, my records had gone gold. I had misread *manslaughter* and mistaken that word for *gold*.

"Catching up on the news?" said Ike Senior behind me, causing me to drop the bottle. It crashed with a thud on the porch floor and spilled.

"I'm telling Clara your elephant plan," I said.

"My plan to give them my money?"

"To sell Gracie's tusks."

"That was a ruse, to test how evil you find me."

"Then it's a redundant ruse."

"I was hoping we had a future."

"You and me both, Dad."

"But you believe I would hurt those elephants."

"Fool me twice," I said, pulling out the phone.

"Well, I've fooled you more than twice, Junior."

I could hear an engine approaching. We both turned to see a police car pull up in the ditch. A tall black man in a fedora got out, the poker player from before.

"Am I interrupting?" he said as he strode toward us.

"What's this about?" said Ike Senior.

"You're harboring a murder suspect, old man."

Here's what I thought, just for a minute: that this cop would earn a bounty from Aisling's father by betraying mine and giving me to the state of Texas. My dad had trusted everyone, even me. In a pinpoint storm's eye I felt glad to know Ike Senior wasn't betraying Clara. But then his inscrutable grin never diminished as the policeman climbed the stairs. It seemed to me that Ike Senior should stop grinning. Before I knew why he didn't, the cop was handcuffing me to the porch railing.

"You can't do this," I said, still expecting my father's smile to wane.

"Turn yourself in, file a complaint," he said, taking the phone out of my other hand.

"How much money?" I said, still believing that the money was because of me.

"News will tell you a thousand per pound," said Ike Senior, "as if there's just one black market in the world. In Beijing you'll fetch close to two thousand."

It hit me, all of a sudden, how dimwitted I'd been to assume there was a bounty. In three days people haven't survived their first stage of grief, let alone set bounties.

"You're monsters," I said.

"My buddy wanted to let you help," Ike Senior said, "but I told him what you're like. You're as bad as that animal rights activist you brought home yesterday."

"Gracie, charge," I shouted, aloud and in my head, screeching like I did in the songs Gracie hated so much.

"He believes Gracie talks to him," said my father.

"She does," I said. "She's smarter than we are."

"That night in New Orleans? I taught you how not to be a mark."

"I blacked it out. What you taught me is to be a drunk."

"You drink too much, that's for sure."

"Why are you doing it?" I asked, but I knew. Because he was good at it. Because of adrenaline. Because of alcohol. He had a lot of nerve, telling me I drink too much.

"They're old and sick," he said. "If you never forgot things, wouldn't you want to die?"

"You said they're like people."

"People, elephants, I roll the same way with all animals. Hey, it's in the blood. You think I didn't know all along why you're here?"

"Why am I here?"

"I've done stuff in my day, Junior, but leaving her to die? That was low."

As my father stepped down from the porch, I was speechless, but only in my voice. Not in my head. *Flee,* I shouted to Gracie in my head as Ike Senior led his buddy toward the garage. *Charge the fence. Tell your friends.* Except she wasn't answering me anymore.

My father and his partner emerged with two automatic rifles apiece and crossed into the sanctuary. They disappeared over the rise. I was working my handcuffs down the railing. When they were low enough for me to kneel, I leaned forward and caught my breath. Now I could relax a little. It was during that spell of calm that I came up with my final song, which never made it onto the album. I didn't get a chance to write it down. It's about regular elephants, not vampires. It takes place fifty years from now, in the year 2062. In it, the computers of 2062 learn to decipher the part of elephant speech that's too low for human ears. Although elephants are extinct by then, videos of them remain online. In my last song the citizens of my future play elephant videos one by one, as their computers translate, and it's like finding ten thousand Anne Frank diaries; the people weep over those staggering words and say, "We wouldn't have let that happen." The African videos are bad enough, with their desperate cries while gunmen mow down elephants from helicopters, but the worst come from Arkansas, from the sanctuary, where every old lady brings her own history of exquisite torture to the watering hole and compares notes with the other cows there, puzzling out what's next.

I succumb to something like postpartum depression after writing a good song, but in that moment, listening for the first gunshot, it felt nice to finish one. I heard the distant wail of another siren. No, no, no, I thought, because as awful as Gracie's fate was, I had quit feeling sorry for myself. It faded, the siren. For a few seconds before it picked up again, I felt proud of not screwing up. I would stay free. If Ike Senior was dealing in ivory, he could smuggle me across the border with my songs. No one would steal the songs, not that I'd guessed yet that anyone would try. I was in luck. I supposed it derived from my having inherited my father's inscrutable poker face, which girls called enigmatic. Most of them couldn't get enough of it. Not just girls, but critics, too. Critics sought my answers, trusted that they were full of subtext. Comment on the metaphorical structures in your songs, the critics would say to me, and I would reply, "There aren't any."

BETSY FROM PIKE

THE MEDIA WOULD REPORT that the teenage Satanist rest-area murderers all hailed from Letcher County, but Betsy grew up in the Daniel Boone Trailers in bordering Pike County. When she was young, her neighbor Jimmy would sing a ballad that went, *Don't you remember Sweet Betsy from Pike? Who crossed the wide mountains with her lover Ike.* Daily Jimmy crooned its verses about Sweet Betsy, her lover, their cattle, their rooster, their pets. He said he'd written it about his sweetheart. He sang it while Betsy rocked on the bench swing, waiting for her ma Irene to get done relaxing. Irene's boyfriend, Floyd, would call to her when they were done, and Betsy would come running, because she loved Floyd, or she did until Irene soured up on them like a jug of milk. Her ma used to toss meat to the three-legged dog, laugh as it galloped toward the meat; now she quit emerging, took to sleeping through the days. One day Floyd tried to rouse her and she said, "It's daylight, dipshit."

"Let's see a doctor."

"Let's leave me be."

"Love you, Irene."

"Get out of my face," Betsy's ma said into her pillow, at which point Floyd decided she wasn't inside herself anymore.

"Find her some help," he told Betsy, packing up his things, and then Betsy quit being inside herself too.

Floating high above their farewell hug, she could see ten trailers and across the mountain into Letcher County. From such height she could hardly ask for Floyd to take her along, or say, "Be my dad," as he drove away from Kentucky. She was twelve and a half. After a long trance like her ma's, she left her bedroom to find Jimmy, her singing neighbor, on the couch.

"Your ma's still in bed, Sweet Betsy, and Floyd's in Tampa," Jimmy said, his glassy eyes fixed on Betsy's chest.

"I'm off to Tampa myself."

"Not if I cut off your legs," he drawled, so languidly that Betsy didn't begin to shriek until he was up and tackling her.

Ma will come, she kept telling herself as Jimmy tugged at her T-shirt, smelling of Cheetos and motor oil, but the door stayed shut. She gave up struggling enough for him to unzip her jeans and touch her down there, saying, "That's all I wanted. Does it feel okay?"

It felt like the cops might come drag her away. To prepare, Betsy locked her mind in jail, where she sewed, wore stripes, played ball, until jail was tolerable enough to let Jimmy kiss her. "I've liked you forever," he said. Next morning he strapped Irene into the car and drove her to the state hospital. He leased his trailer to a mechanic. He moved in with Betsy, signed drop-out-of-school forms, put her on Depo-Provera, called her his belle, and so on like that for some years until Betsy awoke one day from a nap and a dream, tied a rope round the neck of the three-legged dog, and walked it down the river gorge to the vet clinic.

Behind the counter at the clinic stood a pale boy whose dyed hair matched his black jeans and black turtleneck. "Need this fellow put down," Betsy said to him.

"Name?" asked the boy, looking weak and skinny enough to be overpowered. Betsy glanced to the stump of the dog's missing leg. In the dream, she had been injecting kids at her school with euthanasia drugs, and now she planned to steal a shot of pentobarbital to use on Jimmy before driving to Florida.

"Tricycle," she said.

"Sorry about that."

"He's seventeen, plus cancer."

"It'll be a few more minutes."

The dog was sniffing around at Betsy's feet. What was its real name? "Hamburger," her ma used to shout at it, in a voice fading from her memory. Would the shot work faster in Jimmy's heart or in his neck, she was wondering when the boy said, "Grab Tricycle."

She carried the dog into an exam room. The gruff, alert woman across the table had only to eye it before Betsy saw that her plan would fail. They know, she thought, readying herself for jail once more, but the vet produced a needle, swabbed the dog's leg, and whispered, "Poor sweet thing."

Stroking the dog with one hand, she stuck it with the other. It began to gasp. "That's just agonal breaths," the vet said; "don't worry."

Betsy wanted to retort that she wasn't fretting about some dog, but she kept quiet until it was over. Back in the lobby the boy asked her for money. "Ain't got none," she said.

"Did you think it's free?"

She shook her head. She hadn't considered the matter at all.

"Have you got a boyfriend?"

"Sort of," she said, feeling cowardly again. Jimmy had sprung back to life in her mind.

"I'll bill you later if you dump that dude and go with me."

Figuring he was making fun of her, she said nothing.

"My name's Austin. You a Christian?"

Betsy had never set foot in church, but Floyd was a Methodist, Ma a Baptist, and Jimmy Church of God. "I ain't anything."

"Your dog died so I could meet you. You scared of Satanists?"

"Guess not," said Betsy, ready for anything that saved her from walking home.

"Then how about our date?"

"Okay," she said, bringing Austin trotting around the counter. He propped her chin in his finger. She clenched up, but to her surprise it felt nice. He tasted of clove smoke. As he breathed heat into her body, she trembled at the energy amassing inside her. She didn't worry about the cops nabbing her, not even as Austin drove them over into Letcher County, to a brick ranch house at the foot of a ridge.

In the den of that place lay two black-haired girls, one fat and one thin, playing a shoot'em-up video game. "My new friend from Pike County," Austin said to them.

A boy on the couch, thirteen or so, his hair also black, turned to look, but the girls didn't budge from their bean bag. "What makes you a Satanist?" asked the fat one, facing the TV.

"Ain't sure," Betsy said.

"Are you one? Tell the truth."

"I'm one cause of the men around here, and Helen too," said the skinny girl, pausing her game so she could indicate the fat girl.

"I'll do what you say."

"Listen," the skinny girl said, now scrutinizing Betsy. "Five dudes from my stepdad's road crew up in Beefhide. Afterward he wouldn't quit the job, my mom wouldn't leave, and they all go to the Church of God. Who's God's enemy?"

Betsy understood to reply, "Satan."

"So what makes you a Satanist?"

"He lives with me. His name's Jimmy."

"We'll add him to our list. I'm Wendy."

"I'm Zacky," the couch boy said.

"Pleasure," Betsy said, and it was. They wouldn't be telling their names if she couldn't stay. Hopeful that the worst had passed, she hugged Austin's neck. He squeezed her back. And when Wendy said, "You're safe," she nearly sobbed aloud at how easily she and the Satanists might never have met.

They fed Betsy ice cream, then got out a legal pad and read out some names. There were schoolkids, teachers, cousins, doctors, cops, an Exxon clerk who'd banned them from his store. Get your nasty asses out, that man had said, for which he would die. Was Betsy okay with it? She nodded. "Prove it," the fat girl said.

"That's Helen," Wendy said again.

"The dog I put to sleep today wasn't mine."

"At Austin's vet?"

"It wasn't even sick. It had three legs, but I was stealing the shot to use on Jimmy."

"Listen, I said you're safe here, but only if we're safe. Cops want us gone."

"I don't mind," Betsy said, without stopping to think.

"Then you can be one of us," Wendy said. "Prepare for your ceremony."

Betsy let herself be led outside. The others gathered in a circle. Night was falling on the hollow. Austin and Zacky lit lighters whose flames obscured the ground, giving Betsy a sense of hovering in space. "In the name of Satan," they all intoned, as she shook with relief, "ruler of earth, chief of the serfs, I command the dark to bestow its power," and so forth, straight on into Lucifer's vow, growing louder, while up the valley a coyote screamed back at them like some organic siren.

The next day Wendy drove Betsy to the Save-A-Lot in Whitesburg for hair dye. Back at the house she applied it to Betsy's hair during her soap operas. She lent Betsy one of her black shirts and one of Austin's. Betsy was hoping to learn more chants, but there weren't any. Zacky showed her how to play *Tomb Raider*. When Austin got home, he snuggled up to her on the carpet. Breathing to match his breath, she tried her best not to move until dinner, frozen pizza, which they ate on the couch during *Buffy*.

"What's the plan for tomorrow?" Betsy asked after a while.

"What do you mean?" Austin said.

"Like what will we do?"

"I've got my work."

"I mean long-term. Tomorrow, but also in general."

"If you want," said Wendy, "you can fly to the moon, but we're staying put."

Later, in his room, Austin let Betsy keep her clothes on and even slept in his own clothes, "So I won't have to bother with it in the morning."

"Do you like your job?" she asked.

"I wish I were a girl so I could stay home for *All My Children*."

"So you're saving up money?"

"Saving for what?"

"I'm asking you. Like for school?"

"No, I'm thinking I'll just hop trains." His words were slow and measured, as if he'd weighed the merits of trains against the merits of school.

"Can you still do that?"

"No law against it. How do you have fun?"

"Hang out, mostly."

"I'd quit, but Wendy won't let me. She and Helen watch *Days of Our Lives*."

All night under the covers Austin never unclasped her bra. It was the same on the nights after. A few times he pressed Betsy's palm to the blonde fuzz on his belly, but mostly they just cuddled. She came to feel safe with him, and she liked the faraway burn of his wide eyes; still, it wasn't long after she'd denied Jesus the deceiver that she decided her new boyfriend was stupid.

He didn't know who the president was. Nor did he know his own parents' names or their ages. What bothered Betsy was how he didn't even mind. She'd dropped out herself, but she still wondered stuff, like what came before the beginning of time? Austin said he'd never considered that. He thought Tennessee was a part of Kentucky. There used to be Indian cities where you could ride around on mammoths; he didn't care. He tried to suck milk out of her breasts, complained when there was none. "Can I ask you something?" he said one morning in bed.

"Shoot," said Betsy.

"How often do you think. . ." He seemed to trail off.

"How often do I think what?"

"No, how often do you think?"

"Like per minute?"

"Like how many times."

"It's hard to count."

"For real?" he asked, which was when Betsy began to fall out of love. Not just with Austin. Back when Wendy had first spoken about the road crew, she'd struck Betsy as wise. Now, after days on end of her pulling Helen's hair over nothing, smacking her for winning video games, she seemed compulsively violent. Every dinner was frozen pizza. Never was there a prayer to Lucifer. Afraid that the Satanists might sense her disdain and banish her to Jimmy, she devised plans for mass killings, like gassing the shaft of the Leary Mine.

"Cops?" Wendy retorted.

"We'll kill them too."

"Don't be a moron."

"But the list."

"Satan ain't about killing, it's about power."

"He," said Helen, as if they had a stake in Satan's gender.

"So the list was some joke?"

"If we kill in Kentucky," said Wendy, maneuvering her avatar across a chasm, "we'll get stuck in Kentucky."

"How about Florida?"

"Thousands of miles away," said Austin, reaching his stupid hand toward her. She had only wanted to seem useful. She'd sworn to have her heart torn out should she betray the oath, but no one needed her. She excused herself, not that they cared, and went wandering onto an old goat trail. It climbed to a high meadow where azaleas bloomed red-orange against the green hills. She paused there to take in the vista. Half the men on their list were down below, in a coal mine. A methane explosion could end their lives, but the Satanists were just kids, scared kids without imagination. To worship somebody, even Satan, Betsy believed, you needed a range of imagination.

As if the cops had read her mind, a siren came slicing through the valley, its wail alien to a landscape whose only manmade sight was their house. It slowed, became stationary. Run and hide, she was thinking when the house burst into flame.

Perplexed, she sat down on a rock. It was spreading quickly. Do something, she thought, poking at a skin of clay coating the rock, but she couldn't remember how you prayed to Satan. Were her friends burning alive?

When the siren fell silent, she heard only crackling flames, tree limbs in the wind.

It occurred to her why the fire had metastasized so fast: the cops had arrested the Satanists for arson, and only then had they doused the place in gasoline.

Strangely empty of fear, Betsy hiked down the opposite side of the ridge. In the valley, where the trail met the road, she came to a place called Beech's Store.

"Seeking a ride to Florida," she told the Mayfield Dairy man.

"Anything for you," the milkman said, letting her into his truck. He drove them onto the highway. "Hear about that fire?" he said.

"Ain't from these parts."

"Devil worshipers burned their house to a crisp."

They were coming into a steep gorge. "Why do they worship the devil?" Betsy asked, keeping watch on the man's reflection while her eyes followed the river.

"Who knows, but those kids have been lurking for years. Fire was God's blessing."

"Huh." A blessing, thought Betsy, taking stock of his hanging cross, his Jesus fish, his John 3:16 sticker. Red dots on the radar detector were blinking as if in code. Something didn't seem right. "Why's the river going upstream?" she asked, reorienting herself to realize they were traveling north into the Kentucky hills again.

"Like I'm driving to Florida with a truck of milk," said her driver, chuckling as if Betsy was a holy fool.

"Stop," she demanded, right at the Pike County line, so that when he did coast to a halt, it was at the foot of the drive leading to the Daniel Boone Trailers.

•

Gazing up that eroded slope, Betsy could see the bench swing, her bedroom window, and Jimmy's Dodge Daytona. Full of the adrenal fear that had been wearing her down ever since her pa had split, she decided to steal that car from Jimmy. Upon her vow, the dread didn't recede. I'll never return, she swore, standing in place, but still it surged. I'll be just a few minutes. I'll shoot Jimmy with his rifle, and that did it; now she could wend her way uphill, recalling memories of Pa. Turnip had been his name. He spoke Québécois French, assembled clocks for fun, worked at the hardware store until one day he up and quit. Could it be he'd grown tired of missing his soaps? There was one in particular; had it been *All My Children*? "You're mocking me," Irene had replied, reaching for the cast-iron skillet, which she hefted and swung into Turnip. He slumped over, blood trickling out of his temple onto one of his clocks. "I'll do worse," Irene threatened while Betsy ran to the crawlspace, where she hid while her father staggered off toward Canada.

At the top of the hill Betsy found Jimmy squinting at her from beneath the Daytona. His shirt was drenched in oil. "Know what you did to Alpha," he said.

Betsy froze. "That dog had cancer," she said, vibrating with fear as Jimmy scooted out from under the car.

"I could send you to prison."

"I'll find you a new dog."

"No, Betsy, take a load off. You're a sight for sore eyes."

To call her by her name worked like a voodoo spell. She took a seat on the swing. "I don't like black hair," Jimmy said.

"Sorry," she said.

"It's all right. We've missed each other."

He sat down next to her and leaned in. The scent of his deodorant, along with the pattern of the electric lines, sent Betsy to the brink of breakthrough after breakthrough. The timing increased along with Jimmy's little kisses. It was her first spell of what the prison nurse would call a form of epilepsy. The déjà vu was the prodrome; the seizure was when her memories vanished entirely. Afterward she awoke in Jimmy's arms as if the Satanists had been a colossal dream. In some valley there'd been a fire, but when; why?

Jimmy was hugging her. "Tired of Pop-Tarts. Fix me breakfast."

At the window, frying sausage, Betsy found no eyes meeting hers from the windows of other trailers. No one was out there. "If I betray my oath," she murmured, "bury me in ocean sand in an eternity of oblivion," but this already felt like oblivion. The trailer court was called Daniel Boone because its residents had died in the 1800s and the remains were a fool's daydream. She shook off that uncanny fear and thought, Jimmy calls me pretty, wants me near. Was it selfish not to love him back? Had she confused him with something else? I'll flee tomorrow, but not today, and not today, and not today, until day thirty, when a judge released the Satanists from detention. Betsy was frying the morning meat again when she saw them climbing the drive to fetch her: Austin, Wendy, Helen, Zacky, the neighbors' pit bulls roaring at them as they took in the squalor.

Before they could knock, she opened the door. "We're going to Florida," said Wendy, skinnier than ever. Helen had gained ten pounds.

"We're in trouble and so are you," Helen added, crowding onto the little porch beside Wendy and holding her hand.

"How's your ma?" said Austin, as Betsy backed inside, ashamed of her home.

"Ma lives in Frankfort."

"With Jimmy?" asked Wendy, following her in.

"You remember Jimmy's name?"

"Those cops read us our list a thousand times."

"That could be any Jimmy," Betsy said, suddenly afraid. The heading had read *MEN WE WILL KILL SOON*.

"Is that him?" said Zacky, pointing to the woods, where Jimmy was emerging holding a rabbit by its ears. A bullseye of blood stained its puffy cottontail.

"We don't want any," he told the Satanists, pushing past them into the trailer.

"Betsy's leaving with us," said Wendy, as Jimmy kissed Betsy on the mouth.

"Oh, you're the ones burned your house down."

"Sheriff burned it in case we turned him in," said Helen.

"I know you by your hair. Turn him in why?"

"For touching me, for starters."

"Wouldn't touch you for all the gold in Fort Knox."

"Your bunny pooped," said Zacky.

They all glanced to see turd pellets dripping out of the rabbit. "What gun you shoot it with?" said Wendy, as she drew a revolver out of her jeans pocket.

She aimed the weapon at Jimmy's chest. He stepped closer. "Look, shithead, I pay for her ma's hospital," he said, as if Irene didn't belong to the indigents' ward. As if Betsy should care one way or the other. She should feel no fonder of her ma than of Jimmy; still, she listened to the oil boiling and pictured a blind man clawing at his eyes. The notion grew into a scene: oil on fire, trailers on fire, her friends falling to their knees in admiration. With heat in her heart, she crossed to the stove, singing, *Good-bye, Pike County, farewell for a while. We'll come back again when we've panned out our pile.*

"Your voice is lovely," Austin said.

Startled out of her will, she backed away from the skillet. The song had seemed a proper thing for Jimmy to ponder in his last moments of sight, but a glimpse of Austin's naïve face reminded her there were others casting their lot with her. Let sleeping dogs lie.

"Breakfast done yet? I'm starved."

Betsy extinguished the flame. "Have at it," she told Jimmy, heading for the door.

"You do construction?" Wendy asked.

"Disability," she heard Jimmy reply as she walked outside.

"But you worked the Beefhide crew?"

"Wasn't gonna say in front of your friends."

"So you know me by my hair."

"Be calm," said Jimmy, just before the shot rang out.

There was a ghostly echo as Betsy spun around. From the porch she could see only a toppling silhouette, but she knew Jimmy was dead before he thumped to the carpet. What if he really had been paying for the hospital? What if they shoved Irene into an alley?

Make it okay, Betsy prayed, choking on a scream, because what if Jimmy had been her soul mate?

"We vowed to kill or tear our hearts out," Wendy said, as if to explain it.

"You told us that was just words," Austin said.

"Everything's just words. What was that song?"

"Jimmy wrote it about me," she managed to reply. "It's called 'Sweet Betsy from Pike.'"

"I like it," Wendy said, leading the way outside. "It's got a nice melody. Maybe you can teach it to me on our way to Florida."

•

In the Daytona they coasted downhill into Letcher County, Helen at the wheel. She braked in every curve. No one spoke. They siphoned gas near the old train depot. It didn't feel to Betsy like Austin was sitting next to her. She felt prohibited from asking how the group had found her, or how they'd gotten to Pike County. The Satanists weren't people you asked questions of—which was why, when she'd seen them coming, she'd planned to join them only as far as the state line. How to admit, now that they were passing Cumberland High, that she'd decided to return to school? She wanted curious friends. Pull over, she thought. Let me out on the left. It had happened before. She tried to recall how it had turned out then, or was it several times, speeding into the Cumberland Gap Tunnel, blinking, wishing, clasping Austin's hand, wishing again, holding her breath through the tunnel so the wish would come true.

Did they take 25E? Did she sing again? Had Wendy meant her praise of the song? Where had they found the gun? Who else did they admit to killing? She would be asked and asked, but the drive through Tennessee was one long blank spell; her only memory was of a memory, along with the church marquee that jogged it. *Submission to God is your softest pillow.* In the induction ceremony, that first night, she'd lowered herself onto dewy grass while the Satanists held their lighters high. To lie under those flames had felt like floating in space. She'd flinched for pain that never came. Peace as she thanked her new god by all his names. "Finally, I swear to kill," she'd said at the oath's end, noticing a shift in diction, as if Wendy had penned that last line but copied the rest from a book.

Hours must have passed. When she awoke, she stood at a rest area studying a map of Tennessee's scenic highways. It was dark, her head ached, and Austin stood behind her, hands round her waist.

"I spaced out a minute," she said, smelling sausage again, while Jimmy's shadow fell and the body crashed.

"You was saying about the difference between Tennessee and Kentucky."

She gestured to the map, shuddering to think she'd nearly used the skillet the way her ma had. "There's Tennessee, and there's Kentucky."

"I'm named after Texas."

"That's a different map."

"You think I'm a retard?"

"Well, Tennessee ain't Kentucky."

Austin went wandering into the night. Alone, Betsy measured thumb-lengths south from the middle until a shadow fell over the display. She swiveled to face a pretty woman whose straw-blonde hair touched the collar of her dress.

"Hello, how are you?" the woman said.

"Okay," she replied with a gulp.

"When you were pacing, your gait caught my eye."

Betsy looked around in the dark. Unfamiliar with the word, she had heard its homonym, and she didn't recall pacing.

"How you walk," the woman explained. "Like you're depressed."

"I ain't," said Betsy, sheltering her hands in her coat pockets, which was when she realized she had Wendy's gun.

"So you're headed south? What's your name?"

Betsy was mulling over an answer when Wendy charged out of the ladies' room, Helen in tow, and said, "What's yours, bitch?"

"I'm Claudia Quillen. My husband and I are Jehovah's Witnesses."

"My name's piss off, and we worship Satan."

"Is that why you wear black?" said Claudia, as a handsome man in a corduroy jacket came over, holding the hand of his tow-headed young son. Flanking the man's other side was a pig-tailed girl who called out, "Mommy!"

"Sweetie," Claudia said, "I'm talking to these young women." To the Satanists she asked, "Do you know Jesus?"

"We ain't been introduced," said Wendy.

"In that case, I've got something to show you," said Claudia Quillen, pointing to a minivan parked beyond a picnic shelter where Zacky and Austin were kicking a hacky-sack.

To Betsy's surprise, Wendy followed Claudia into the night. Keeping pace, Betsy trailed a few lengths behind. Trucks were roaring past on the interstate, too distant for any driver to see them looking so shabby, even ugly, beside Claudia and her radiant family. At the van Claudia opened the hatchback, unzipped a suitcase. She took out a book. Austin caught up and held Betsy from behind.

"'If any man come to me,'" Claudia read, "'and hate not his father, and mother, and wife, and children, and brethren, and sisters, yea, and his own life also, he cannot be my disciple.'"

The strange verse seemed tailor-made for the Satanists. It was like she could see into their minds. "So you hate your husband?" said Wendy.

Claudia glanced at Mr. Quillen, who had stopped some distance away. He was smart to guard his children in the shadows, Betsy thought, fearing for those kids herself even as she envied them.

"Daniel and I were loathed by our families."

"Why is that?"

"Honey, strap in the kids?"

"They don't want our help," said Mr. Quillen, but he came and opened the sliding door. As their daughter climbed in, he turned on the stereo. A chorus of children began to sing "Do Your Ears Hang Low," and Claudia kept reading, or reciting, given the path of her eyes from Satanist to Satanist.

"'If ye were of the world, the world would love his own: but because ye are not of the world, but I have chosen you out of the world, therefore the world hateth you.'"

Yes, thought Betsy, it does, but what place was this where mild-mannered strangers gently said so? She was still scouring her mind for memories when Wendy said, "The world doesn't hate you."

"Child, who cares for you?"

"So now I'm a child?"

"You're all children. You've been wounded."

"Ma'am, we care for one another," said Wendy, which was when Betsy knew that the Quillens were in danger. Wendy didn't call people *ma'am*.

She opened her mouth to warn them, but found herself as mute as when she'd passed by the school. "There's only five of you," Claudia said. "A child needs more than four other people to love her."

"How many people loving her does a child need?"

"That's the wrong question to ask."

"Because I've dealt with a lot."

"Just come in the van for a bit."

"That's what I was fixing to do," said Wendy, reaching into Betsy's pocket for the revolver, which she pointed to where the Quillen boy was squirming in the middle seat.

As hysteria broke out around her—Zacky chasing Claudia onto her luggage, Helen running for the driver's door—Betsy counted the times her heart prodded her lungs. She'd picked up some ways to suffer through dread. While the kids were in panic, shouting along with their dad, she measured her pulse. Eighteen per breath. I don't know how the gun got there, she thought in rehearsal, before she was pulled in the side door to crouch by the seat. "Drive," Wendy commanded. Immediately they were bouncing into each other. The girl was shrieking. The tape segued to a chorus of children's voices that sent Betsy to the verge of every lost memory as she heard Claudia beg, "Where are we going?"

"Your song," Wendy said.

She could barely hear it over the engine, the girl, the whistling air, and the whirring of Helen's swerves across the rumble strips. "You know this one?" asked Daniel Quillen, softly, distant, at the far end of a tunnel.

"I don't know any songs," Betsy said, which felt like the truth until the girl fell silent and she could make out the familiar upbeat ballad.

> They soon reached the desert where Betsy gave out
> And down in the sand she lay rolling about
> While Ike in great tears looked on in surprise
> Saying Betsy get up you'll get sand in your eyes.

"She knows it," Wendy said. "It's about the county she comes from."

"You're from Missouri?" asked the girl, speaking for the first time.

"I'm from Pike County, Kentucky," Betsy said, confused. It had to be a trick; Jimmy couldn't have sold her song to the radio.

"Sweet Betsy comes from Pike County, Missouri."

"It's Olivia's favorite song," her father explained. "She researched it."

"It's about Pike County, Kentucky," said Betsy, sensing that there might not be a song about her after all.

"It's about the California Gold Rush. They leave Pike County to pan for gold but they never find it."

"Kentucky didn't have a gold rush," said Austin, to whom Betsy might have snapped back, Do you even know what a gold rush is, except she felt even stupider than Austin. Because if the lover was called Ike, not Jimmy, how had she never realized?

They had left the interstate. On a two-lane road high above a moonlit valley, Betsy felt a touch, and turned to see Claudia Quillen balanced awkwardly on the luggage. "God put you at that rest area," she said, echoing something Betsy had heard before.

It was Austin's notion about the three-legged dog.

"He did it to wake us up. We may be giving our kids a good home, but so many kids are without parents at all."

"We've got parents, fuckwad," Wendy said, as if she too felt affronted by the idea of fate. The euthanasia shot, the fire, Irene, Jimmy, all of it meant to be.

"I don't blame you for hating God. What do your parents do?"

"My dad's on a construction crew," Wendy said.

"And your mother?"

"Ain't talking about Mom."

"Tell me about your mom."

"Ain't nothing worth telling."

"If your parents don't love you, that's unfair," said Claudia, louder, seeming to speak to everyone at once. "You can't feel God's love until you've felt normal love."

"I didn't say they don't love me."

"Sweetie, do you wonder what existed before time?"

"No," said Wendy, as Betsy trembled again with the shock of déjà vu. It wasn't a seizure this time, but a real memory of asking Austin the same question. How could nothing exist? How was forever possible? He had merely shrugged, but Claudia said, "Earth is a billion times bigger than Tennessee. The solar system's a billion times bigger again. The galaxy's a billion times bigger again, and the universe? It grew out of a single grain of sand."

As if in awe at such enormity, Claudia gazed into the dark. The Satanists were silent. Maybe their minds were boggling like Betsy's, sagging like slack ropes.

"Do you want to know how?"

"Yes," said Betsy, as her song came to an end.

"Because God wanted it this way."

"But what came before God?"

"What do you mean?"

"How did it all start?"

"That's why we pray," said Claudia, and Betsy's mind quit boggling, because Claudia was no more curious than the Satanists.

She was paging through her Bible again. That fire was God's blessing, Betsy recalled the milkman saying. Claudia's reason wasn't a reason. Betsy imagined Jimmy in church thanking the Lord. "I'm grateful for my life," Jimmy had told the Lord, when his life was Betsy. An infinite universe, while she'd spent years in a trailer, seeing none of it. Now the Satanists were listening to this drivel without any argument. Had Claudia worn them down? Betsy saw them in happy worship together, the Satanists and Quillens, singing hymns. Only she shivered alone in the dark outside the Kingdom Hall. The tables had turned against her, unbearably against her, it seemed, until Wendy drew the revolver.

A sweet thrill brimmed inside Betsy. It wasn't because she wanted to cause harm. For Claudia Quillen to live a thousand years would have been fine with Betsy. The gun meant she wasn't alone. Like Betsy, Wendy was balking at a doctrine that called their misery God's desire. To the two of them, nothing was a blessing. As if to confirm it, Wendy glanced at her. For a moment, even after Wendy pulled the trigger and shot Claudia in the heart, Betsy thought she was learning that she and Wendy loved each other.

Blood poured out of Claudia, soaking her shirt. Betsy saw it in the periphery as she held Wendy's gaze. She heard Olivia scream and Daniel moan. The van coasted to a halt. Through the whole spate of violence—Zacky seizing the gun and shooting Daniel, then drawing it on Olivia, finally forcing the cocked weapon into Helen's hands and commanding, "Your turn"—neither Wendy nor Betsy blinked.

The shot blasted the girl halfway out of her seat. "Now give it to Betsy," Zacky said, as the boy choked.

"No," Austin said, blocking her from Helen's reach.

"We've all got to, to make it equal."

"She done killed her dog," said Austin, who must have thought he was saving her life. Betsy didn't want her life saved. What she wanted was Wendy's love. She hadn't understood that until now. If it meant worshiping Satan, so be it. "Give it," she said, taking the gun from Helen. Aiming it at the Quillen boy, she looked at Wendy again. I love you, she thought, before realizing her error.

The mistake wasn't to love, but to admit to the love in her mind. She'd chased Floyd off that way, and Turnip too. Even her ma. She was repulsive to them all, and sure enough, even Wendy blinked and turned away.

Austin squeezed Betsy's thigh. They were coming to a truss bridge. He only liked her because she didn't want him—and why not, now that she knew she was stupid too? She couldn't remember an hour ago. For all she knew, they could be crossing back into Pike County again. Driving to Florida with a truck of milk. How often did she think? Of course Jimmy hadn't written that song.

She pictured his smirks after he came, as if he wished she would shrivel to nothing. Déjà vu was when she lived out the things that had happened to her ma. Before long she would get pregnant, turn mean, go to bed, and a neighbor would commit her to the state hospital.

High above a river, Austin said, "Let me," offering his life for hers, which struck Betsy as his dumbest move yet.

There was a hiss as the cassette switched sides. "Oh, my darling, oh, my darling," sang the children as Claudia let out a few last sputters. That's just agonal breaths, Betsy thought. It began to dawn on her what they had done. She wasn't fully a part of it yet, nor was Austin, who stared with dumb, adoring eyes. Hope dwindling, she watched for a similar sign from Wendy. None came. Figuring she had one last chance for it, she fired, which jerked her with enough force that the Quillen boy took his bullet off-center and lived through to the trial that would rivet both Kentucky and Tennessee the next spring.

For years after the journalists gave up, the chaplain at the Tennessee Prison for Women kept probing: Do you hate Austin for what he testified? Will he never come visit you? Do you still love him? Did you kill for love? Why'd you think killing would make somebody love you? And how did it feel when Jimmy sent your ma away? It must have burned you up. You must have dreamed of murder, even way back then.

The reporters had hoped she would reply, "Yes," whereas the chaplain wanted, "I was just a kid, and Jimmy ruined me," so he could go, "Christ forgives!" She said nothing. The other Satanists had blurted whatever they could think of, but Betsy talked only in her head. To both Satan and Jehovah, she prayed for mental illness to set in. When it didn't, she began to research other faiths' devils and gods. The books she read led her to studies further and further afield. After a few years, she had given herself the equivalent of a high school education. Still, she never could seem to pray right. She would stroke the place between her eyes that some religions called the third eye, petting it with a finger, begging for a spirit to push through. None did. For her ma never to have taken her to church, not once, came to seem like child abuse. Even Floyd, a Methodist, had attended service alone. She discussed that with no one, but she touched herself often, until one bright day in the courtyard when the chaplain said, "What's with your head?"

"I'm trying to go crazy like my ma."

"By rubbing your head?"

"Spirits enter through your third eye."

The chaplain touched Betsy's forehead. "I see what's wrong."

"What?" said Betsy.

"There's a hymen over your third eye."

"Oh, can you fix it?"

Frowning, he flicked that spot with a finger. "One way to find out," he said, and jabbed Betsy so hard there that she fell over backward.

Before she could take in enough air to yell for help, he was on top of her. "Witch! Devil!" he cried out, hammering into her third eye with five joined fingers until a guard came and said she'd had enough.

The two men walked away. Pain radiated through Betsy. "All right?" asked an inmate. Lying there on the lawn, she shook her head. Something was happening. It was as though spirits were pouring in, guiding her toward a vision of the future. She could see a van crossing a river. Bloody Jimmy with his bunny. The house fire, the soap operas. A vet's office. A swing. It overwhelmed her like the sunlight, until she understood: in prison the future was just memories. She barely had any. All her life she'd been forgetting so much. Look how little she recalled of Jimmy's years. In her mind they hardly comprised a week. A gnaw of dread; a few verses of a song. What a fool she'd been, praying for oblivion when it was already hers. The future was the past in mirror image, nothing else to it. You've always been providing, she thought, rolling over onto her belly to shade her eyes.

BUGABOO

I FIRST MET MAX ON my way home from the Gulp, a bottomless whirlpool in the Everglades where people go to commit suicide. This was in 2005. You have to hike six miles along a blackwater canal dug by Andrew Jackson's slaves to a remote lake where you wade out until you're sucked under to drown. Your body turns up in the Intracoastal Waterway. I don't know the physics of it.

For hours I stood on the pier girding myself, even threw my phone into the water, but then I chickened out and didn't squeeze between the rails. I walked back along Jackson Ditch. Twilight was fading when I reached my truck again, miles into the swamp on a road I hadn't known was gated until I found myself locked in.

To the left the grade dropped off into the canal ditch. To the right stood a tarpaper shack whose fence blocked the path I might have driven across.

My only choice was to kill the engine, walk to the porch, and ring the bell. Almost immediately a middle-aged obese man opened the door holding a bottle of Johnnie Walker.

"I'm locked in," I said to him.

"They shut that gate," he replied, gesturing not toward it but to the night itself, which had closed in on the horizon.

"What can I do?"

"I'll fetch the number."

"My phone's dead."

"Use mine," he said, beckoning me into his home. I followed him into a dim room where some hard drives blinked green under a long table full of computer monitors.

"You a programmer?"

"Work for the government. Name's Max."

"That's my name too," I said. "What branch?"

"Guess. And sit."

After I lowered myself into a chair, his screens came alive with satellite feeds of cities, plains, and, in the far right, a pier poking into water. On it stood a guy who looked like a skillet from overhead, his arm stretching out from a circle of black hair.

It was me, right after I'd thrown my phone into the lake.

"Care to see a movie I did?" said the other Max, hitting play already as he spoke.

The video feed showed a girl plunging from the pier into neck-deep water. Her shimmering hair floated behind her as she waded toward the Gulp, which swallowed her, leaving only rings of waves.

Max increased the playback speed. Hand in hand a decrepit white-haired couple scurried to their deaths, followed by more girls.

"What is this place?"

"I spy for the CIA on other countries," said Max, as a parade of suicides continued dying for us under clear skies. Now he summoned up feeds where nude men and women sunbathed on a beach, an orgy of men sucked each other off by moonlight, and

two shoeless women trudged across a desert full of yellow flowers. I took those two for refugees until one bent over to suck on the
other one's nipple.

"Get a load of this," said Max.

I expected another video, but he poured me a scotch.

"I don't drink," I said.

"How long?"

"Four and a half years."

"And she still won't take you back?"

"Who won't?" I said, uneasy.

"The girl you love." He pressed the drink into my hand.

I couldn't help but close my fingers around it. "This stuff was
ruining my life."

"It ever drive you to kill yourself?"

"Worse," I said, breathing in the peaty smell. Already I could
taste smoke on the lips of some of the girls I'd kissed while drunk.
I put the glass to my mouth. What dread I'd had was flushed out
by the whiskey that flowed into me and felt right. "Worse like
how?" Max said, a question it felt possible to address now that I
had liquor in me, so I began by explaining that he was right about
the girl, Livia, whom I'd met on Coulter Mountain in my third year
of recovery.

The first year, when I got back into climbing, I didn't plan on
free-soloing. I just hated speaking to people while I was sober.
To find belaying partners, you had to talk to them. As for rope-
soloing, I had too much anxiety in those days to move so slowly.
Slower I moved, the more my head twitched. So one day I just left
my ropes and Grigri in the car. About halfway up a 5.11, I realized
I wasn't anxious. Clinging to the rock I felt supernaturally good,
like I was part of the earth's mechanics. At the summit I vowed to

climb that way from then on. For two years, I did. By the time I hoisted myself onto the dome of Coulter Mountain with no gear but chalk, I'd forgotten I had ever been ill.

On top of that cliff I rolled over onto my back and looked around. Cross-legged toward the view sat a hot girl in a sports bra, drinking something green out of a Nalgene.

"Did you just free-solo this mountain?" she said.

"For *Rock and Ice*," I answered, which was true: *Rock and Ice* wanted a piece on how free-soloing helped keep me on the wagon.

"If you were writing about suicide, would you drown yourself?"

"No, I'd free-solo K2. Is that a margarita?"

"Yeah," she said, offering it. I shook my head.

"Herradura Gold," she said.

"Sounds delicious," I said.

"Let me guess, free-climbing's the next best thing to alcohol? A pure vertical dance? Like leaping on the moon?" She was quoting a climber named Brendan Timmins who had recently died doing it. "Think of his mother, think of his siblings."

. "Brendan was an only child."

"Which makes his shit even more selfish."

Without the endorphins lingering from my climb, I'd have been too timid to say, "Back when I chose to free-solo, I didn't have you to live for."

"So I'm saving your life?"

"Teach me how to use ropes."

"You're asking me out?"

"Feels like a date already."

"Will you mention me in your article?"

"If you sign an exclusivity contract," I said. We flirted like that for a while. It didn't take me long to see her point: if I had died,

I'd never have lowered her behind the summit's cairn and kissed her. After a climb it's so effortless to pick out what you want, and ask for it. I said so in my *Rock and Ice* essay, which Livia wept over. I wrote how, when I drank, I never trusted that I deserved anyone. Now that a smart woman who climbed fourteeners let me live with her, it felt like no small cozy miracle. I promised in print not to free-solo ever again. Livia is what comes of sober focus, I wrote, as if that along with my climbing had spawned a third, better accomplishment.

I couldn't stay away from her. I would come sit in her photography classes, help with shoots. I took up trail running so we could do the Colorado Trail together. When my delusions started coming back, I hoped they were only a byproduct of love. Sometimes when I fell prey to daydreams where she was bludgeoned and I was the suspect, or where her brakes failed after rusting out from road salt that I'd forgotten to hose off from her truck's underbelly, I drove to the canyon without my gear and scrambled up as far as the death line. Up there at that height, ropeless, I could quit fearing that Livia would die by my inadvertent hand. Perched on crumb-sized knobs I felt as if all history, plate tectonics, evolution, had conspired to bring me a peace I could tap into in secret, once or twice a week, until Livia finished her MFA and got a job offer from a Miami art school.

With no idea how it would feel, I told Livia I'd go anywhere. We moved into an apartment in Hialeah beside a sixteen-lane highway, five hundred miles south of the nearest hill. The temperature was always seventy indoors, one hundred outdoors. I found a job at a rock gym, where I taught kids how to tie knots and brooded my way into a full-on mood disorder.

It began with little things, like driving over a bump, then obsessing over the idea that the bump had been a person. I would scour the news for evidence of a hit-and-run. At the gym some guy would fall onto the mat, and visions of a criminal investigation would plague me. I grew scared to strap kids into their harnesses lest they accuse me of touching them. The sound of any siren suggested that Livia was dead and the cops were coming. The more unlikely the idea, the harder I obsessed.

"Do you ever dread stuff that will never happen?" I managed to ask Livia over coffee one morning. It was the first time I'd mentioned such a thing to her. No matter how she'd balked at free-soloing, I figured she was mine only because her instincts drew her to strength and daring.

"Sometimes I dream you've run off to free-solo Half Dome."

"I mean things that could literally never happen."

"Like you being nice to my friends?" Some of her colleagues had taken us snorkeling in the Keys, hiking in the Everglades, which unfortunately was causing her to enjoy life in Miami. Livia took her new job to get rid of me, I thought later at the gym. By following her to Florida, I had called her bluff. The choice to relinquish mountains was an exam I'd failed. Now she wished for me to go free-solo Half Dome, and fall out, except maybe I had no courage left to climb at all. That's what I was thinking when I realized I could have left the stove on that morning at breakfast.

As unlikely as it seemed, I felt so certain about it that I couldn't bring myself to call Livia. I had already killed her along with a dozen others. No matter the worry's insanity; it consumed me. My stomach roiled, my cheeks burned. Hours later, when I finally did call, she didn't answer.

I was dialing a second time when Ty, the owner of the rock gym, walked in. "I've been ringing you for days," he said.

"The phone was broken. I just fixed it."

"I don't care how good a climber you are; you're fired."

"Okay," I said, nearly thanking him. With pure relief I hurried home to find an intact apartment, where Livia was drinking mimosas with a pixie-faced woman.

I hardly had time to relax before that woman came in toward me for a European-style cheek kiss. Even during my calmest era, studying abroad in Marseilles, deep-water soloing in the calanques, I'd feared these damned gestures, because which side? How many times? Her lips were traveling toward mine as if we were to kiss like lovers—which, since it went so fast, was what I did, giving her the quickest peck.

"So lovely to see you," she said, as if I'd done nothing wrong, but already I could hear the two of them later, cackling with their friends about it.

"Come kayaking with us," said Livia, pouring juice into a champagne glass. The stove was turned off.

"I have to get back to work."

"I was just telling Livia we'll offer her early tenure. We'd hate to lose you."

My arms thrummed with the creep of mercury inside me, as heavy as on a climb. That was it, I thought, I'd fallen and this was my dying dream.

"Max, I showed Mary your magazine pieces. She thinks we can get you a spousal hire in creative nonfiction."

Now the whole scene felt staged. "Cheers," said Mary, clicking glasses to mine. Had they snuck champagne into my drink? I almost hoped so, but booze soothed only healthy brains; what if I drank and my fears lingered?

"Tell me how it feels."

"How what feels?" I said, wondering if she meant anxiety, or being stupid enough to kiss her on the mouth.

"The crazy shit you used to do."

"You stay in the flow without worrying," I said, gripping my glass and swearing to myself that she wasn't flirting, nor would any mothers of young rock climbers be turning me in for child molestation.

"So like yoga, but with the risk of death?"

"It gives perspective."

"Wish I had that kind of mind control."

"You'd be no fun if you did," said Livia, and then they were laughing together and I pretended not to notice how it masked a deeper laughter.

"I should return to work," I said, hurrying toward the door so as to avoid another kiss. What I really did was drive to Key West. It took five hours because I kept pulling over after bumps to verify that no bodies lay in my wake. How I yearned to put that behind me. I'd always thought going crazy meant not knowing it, never feeling it set in. On Key Largo I began brooding over the stove eye. When I'd checked that it was off, had I twisted it too far? So many could perish: retirees, children, infants; then there would be the trial, prison, until I parked on Duval Street and walked the avenues of the village past old men sipping wine. Their little salmon-colored bungalows looked so familiar, but I'd never been here. Livia had come frolicking with her friends one time. It struck me that déjà vu was memories of the future. I had turned away from the past, which was rock climbing; the future was Florida porches because of a girl who'd never desired me to begin with.

Delusion or no, I would feel this way from now on. A mountain might help, but it was impossible to drive so far over so many bumps, farther and farther from proof of dormant stove eyes. Instead I traveled to the Everglades and hiked out to that tree-ringed lake to give myself to the Gulp.

As soon as I'd thrown my phone in, it began to ring. That's

the cops, I thought as it sank into the lake. To destroy evidence suggested guilt, but over what? Livia? Why dread the future here at the brink? If Livia was dead, shouldn't I jump? To regain the serenity to kill myself, I sat down by the water's edge and gazed up the ditch that Andrew Jackson's slaves had dug. Their nearest mountain had stood a month's journey away across deadly country. All their lives they'd labored without knowledge of the prospect a climb offered. Had they climbed trees, at least looked down on the river of glass? Here I was struggling for the wherewithal to breathe. To put my breakdown on hold long enough to die, I thought of all the slaves who'd had no breakdowns, along with slaves in my century. More slaves were alive now than ever. Indentured tomato pickers, miners, young virgins being smuggled out of the Third World, making it through their hardships to carry on.

"You're too connected to your fear receptor," said Max the spy, once I'd brought him up to the present.

Feeling sanguine under the influence, I nodded. He gave me another pour. "But sometimes my receptor shuts up."

"Not sure what you mean."

"I'll show you."

I had him load footage for such and such coordinates for a day I'd crack-climbed a wall in Utah. Suddenly there I was, scrambling ropeless up a red cliff face, the satellite orbiting at a low enough angle that we could watch me pull myself higher. I might as well have been crawling on flat ground, so quickly did I place my fingers on the holds.

"I can see how that would feel tranquil," said Max, without apparent sarcasm.

"Really? You're the first one who's understood."

"Do many die?" he asked.

I gave him another set of coordinates. Soon we could see Brendan Timmins inching up a cliff in Eldorado Canyon. He sped the playback up to 32x, so that in seconds Brendan's grip gave out and he fell backward onto a candlestick spire.

"Spectacular," Max said.

"If you like that, there's plenty more."

"What I like is naked people fucking."

"Go to Half Dome, in Yosemite."

"You go to Half Dome in Yosemite."

"Are you saying kill myself?"

"Were you happy, climbing?"

"Always," I said.

"Then go to Half Dome."

"Will you watch me?"

"If you take your clothes off."

"Deal," I said, offering my hand. We shook on it, then settled back into viewing live-action porn on three screens.

"If you don't die soon, you'll live to see the day when they can scan our brains, take audits of every thought we've ever thought."

"Seems like that's a few years off."

"Depends on your brain. If you let them freeze it when you die, they'll never resurrect you, they'll just hook you up to the audit machine and view a montage."

Normally I'd have been into Max's theory, but I was getting drunk. I floated into imagining a psych student's compare/contrast paper on two brains, my mother's and my own. Cremate her, I told myself, specify cremation in my own will, and so on until I passed out. I came to in my truck camper, lying on the mattress I kept there for climbing trips. The gate to the Jackson Ditch spur had risen, and Max's car was gone. I remembered nothing past the audit machine.

As I pissed into the filthy water of the swamp, my head throbbed so hard I knew I couldn't face Livia. Instead I drove to the beach. Feeling more strung out by the minute, I walked the boardwalk until I came to the kind of wood-paneled, window-less juke joint I used to like. I ordered a bourbon there. Drinking it, I had some thoughts that would be damning in a brain scan, about the fate I wished upon everyone. I thought of my father, who drank daily, and of my cousins on my mother's side who still lived with their parents and hadn't set foot outside in years. I'm not feeling paranoid, I thought by way of appeasing my mind. If I were like my relatives, I'd be paranoid even on whiskey.

At the next bar, a Joe's Crab Shack, a girl split off from her friends to come touch my fingers. "I climb," I said to explain their size.

"Where, Cuba?"

"Wherever there's a mountain."

"You looking for one?"

"You have one in mind?" I said, studying her closely now that she'd asked a smart question. She was perky, spritelike, twenty-one or so. Already I knew I could drive drunk with her over bumps without fear of the bumps.

"There's a rock gym up the road."

"Pretty thing like you must be seeing someone," I said, running a finger along her arm. It would be bliss to ride over the bumps with this girl.

"Boyfriend cheated, so I dumped him," she said, setting us in motion to buy ourselves a room at a beachfront hotel.

It was only afternoon. The hours flew by. At midnight we snuck up to the rooftop pool and took off our clothes. Before I joined her in the water, I turned on the spotlight over the diving board. "No, by moonlight," she said, shielding her eyes.

"But I want to see your body," I replied, which was true. More importantly, I thought Max might have been keeping track of me. I hoped to pay him back for saving my life. "Okay," said the girl, wrapping herself around me. Even knowing I would crawl home alone in shame, I waved happily to the sky. For every moment of it I loved Livia, is the thing, wanted to grow old with her, take her to France to the calanques, where even she could free-solo alongside me because a fall lands you in the sea.

I woke up alone, with enough gin still in me that I didn't dread Livia's verdict yet as I drove home. With mild concern I noticed bumps, laughing at myself a little. The radio news spoke of some Mexican tomato pickers enslaved near Orlando. "I lost my phone," I repeated as I drove, rehearsing my lie until I walked into my home and Livia ran and squeezed me like a harness and said, "I thought you were dead."

"I lost my phone," I said, heart plummeting into my gut.

"It's okay, these things happen."

"I don't remember where."

I waited for her to smell the other girl. Instead she said, "I want to help."

"To what?"

"I'll join you at meetings."

"You hardly drink."

"Every day I drink."

"One margarita with your friends."

"I love you, Max."

I studied her face for a sign of why she wasn't angry. For why she would love me. "I'll try harder," I said, not lying. If there'd been a way to add, "Something's wrong and I need more help than you can give," I'd have done it, but the shock of seeing her had sobered me up. My brain was dividing back into two parts, not hemispheres, but overlapping parts, sort of like air and the Higgs field. The Higgs field isn't the air, but wherever there's air, there's the Higgs field. I'd have explained this, but the energy was pulling me into a maze with all manner of dead ends. "Something's wrong" was one she had predicted in a wager. I kept quiet. The next day, whether or not she believed I was at work, I walked the beach, stopping every few miles for fifty push-ups. My mind felt less urgent if I was moving. Before continuing with fifty sit-ups, I would wave to Max. At sunset I drove home to find Livia reading about some photographer.

"Max, I have a surprise. Is your passport current?"

"Unless you've done something to it."

"You know the Bugaboos?"

"The mountains in British Columbia?"

"You wrote them up for *Rock and Ice*. Mary's cousin has a house there he's not using, near Radium Hot Springs."

"Why the Bugaboos?" I said, playing along.

"I told you. We can go for New Year's."

"So the mountain range?"

"Snowpatch Spire has routes up to 5.12."

"It's just weird you picked it of all places."

"We can do intermediates together."

"But the word *bugaboo*."

"Is that a word?"

"You're smarter than this."

"I know it's a stroller."

"Why do you take pictures?"

"What?" she said, echoing every lying woman in films.

"When you take pictures, other people are taking pictures of you taking pictures."

"You're sounding like your mom."

"People watch us doing the things we do."

"Do you wonder how I know how your mom sounds?"

"The jig is up, okay?" I said, raising my voice. Her book wasn't a photography book. Easy enough to put a fake cover over some maps of neural pathways. But before I could levy my accusation, she cut me off.

"It was eating at me, what you said. I figured, what harm to visit? She talked about you for hours. She's got copies of your articles. Pictures everywhere. Not that it seems pleasant to live in her head," and so on, as it sank in that I must have killed a climber, kicked loose a rock and sent him hurtling to his death. Livia was that climber's sister. Saying she loved me had been the giveaway. At the original ambush she'd gone on about a dead free-soloist, same as she did now about my mom. My mom knitting in a congregate apartment. My mom tearful over losing me. Somehow I lasted through it without taking the bait. Afterward she cuddled up against me in bed, an act no less cynical for her having done it for years. I waited until I heard her snoring, then gathered a sleeping bag, my climbing shoes, a tent.

When I returned for a last look, she was lying on her side, an arm folded across herself. Her scent can't be a disguise, I thought, leaning over to inhale lavender and almond, which brought memories flooding in of years condensed into one day's fever dream. It had felt so real; still, I'd seen this movie, and summoned up the next beat, which was me in my truck driving north onto the Florida Turnpike.

To the tune of a mournful ballad I guzzled Red Bull. The sun rose near Pensacola. When my phone rang—the new one Livia got me—I threw it out. Right away I realized it could cause a wreck. If an overloaded truck ran over it, one that was already struggling to balance, it could tip over. The phone could be traced back. Should

I turn around? After hours of angst about this and about losing the only girl I would love, I pulled over and crawled under the camper to sleep. The next day I woke up and drove twenty more hours. The day after that, I arrived at sunset below the Yosemite climbers' camp.

It was dark when I hiked up to some flat terrain beyond the campground. In the distance dozens of climbers clustered around their campfires while I pitched my tent. Hammering in my final stake, I heard a voice announce, "Max Rainey."

There in the starlight stood a young climber I didn't recognize. "Max Rainey's in Camp Four," he called out.

"Do I know you?" I asked, praying for him to be just some kid. After thousands of miles here I was, stuck in my mind.

"I love your essays. What happened?"

"Have you been watching me?"

"Everyone watches you," he said, as a crowd approached, ten or twelve men masked by the dark and saying, "Dude," "Hey, man," as if I knew them.

"Hey," I replied, wishing they'd get it over with.

"Gonna free-solo Half Dome?" said someone whose voice I nearly recognized.

"Maybe El Capitan," I said.

A few of them laughed. "Where were you?" said the original voice.

"I quit for a girl," I said, figuring I could admit that much even to my enemies. And maybe, unlikely though it was, they weren't enemies. They were putting a lot of effort into pretending to admire me. Follow them to their campfire, I thought; spill my guts and be told relax, she loves you, use our phone, go back. I said no more. Even in my worst hours I've understood that abjectness fails when pitched toward minds that don't throb.

"So if you're back, she's gone?"

"Correct."

"Sorry, dude."

"Join us for s'mores," said someone else, calling my bluff, so that I could only thank him and promise to come later. Really? Sure thing. Awesome. But surely they knew that if I could have joined them, I could have stayed in Florida. They wandered off. I unstaked my tent, moved it deeper into the woods. I lay down. I slept through myriad disturbing dreams that all vanished when I awoke at dawn into the same disquiet, more of it; it was nonsensical how much unease I felt by the time I was hiking to the base of the iconic vertical wall.

If I say I leapt onto the rock, it seems like boasting, but I wasn't scared. Scrambling up a crack, I barely considered my grip on the holds. No, I was counting reasons to be ashamed, and everything I'd said, how each word had been misconstrued. I thought of women I'd mistreated. I could be a father by now, or some girl could have been fifteen. Too many to tally, these fears formed a solid cloud that became my mind until I recalled the other Max.

I dug in, hung back. Although the cliff edge blocked me from half the sky, Max could see me from some satellite.

"I forgot about my clothes," I told him, angling my face up so he could read my lips, and then I glanced down and saw no one below.

It would have been okay to discover someone watching. I'd reached the death line, high enough that the throbbing died down. I could feel it dissipating into the valley. That was why I pulled myself higher. Never had I felt more eager for explicit danger. Gripping the fissures, I climbed into an empty-headedness, euphoric compared to earlier. At one point I rose into a swarm of flies that bit me all at once. What could I do, swat? The pain kept me focused. I thought of shouting for someone to phone Livia, tell her I'd fled for no reason. I counted fly stings, thinking of my body versus the rock, my energy against its inertia, until some gravel fell to either side of me, followed by a body-sized stone.

If there hadn't suddenly been a six-inch ledge to hoist myself onto, I would have died in that earthquake. The whole mountain grumbled hungrily against my belly. Rock after rock fell past me as I stood on the brink, catching my breath. The pause calmed me enough that I became aware of my insane position hundreds of feet above the earth. So I began to gasp. Suddenly I couldn't push air out fast enough. I felt above me for a knob or stirrup. Nothing. Far below, closer to the Merced River than to me, an eagle swooped. I'll die, I thought, soaked in fearful sweat that was my body's shot at saving me. The sweat would make the rocks slippery. In seconds I would die. And then I realized what most people find obvious: This is what fear is for. This is how it feels for fear to work right.

My body had gone haywire, fear when safe, well-being on the verge of death. Down below, no panic of mine had subsided on its own, but here was the answer, a thousand feet high. Hard to take, yet it offered a way out. My actions weren't against the law. No one could prevent me from lifting myself onto fifty-fifty thimbles, as I did then, that is to say a thimble-sized knob with a fifty-fifty chance of holding me. It did. The next one, too. The next one, too, pitch after pitch until I summited that shark's tooth of a mountain, pulled myself over, lay back to see a single wispy cloud drifting toward a faded moon.

"Nuh-uh," said a woman I could have slapped, because already my chemical response was proving my theory true. I wasn't ready for it to resume.

"Give me a minute," I said, without turning to face her.

"USGS is reporting 4.7, but you're crazy under any circumstances."

Now I did look up at this young, wiry climber. Like Livia she was awed, and dumb enough to perceive me as strong. "Your muscles are throbbing," she said, imprinting on me like some turkey poult, as it became obvious: even if Livia did love me, it wasn't for my mind, or my personality. My qualities.

It was bodily instinct, nothing more.

Pushing myself up, I said, "We're not living in caves anymore."

"Beg your pardon?" said the woman, stepping even closer, but I had had more than I could bear.

"This isn't 100,000 BC. You people have got to quit seeking out somebody tough enough to club the lions."

"You might be hypoglycemic," she said, offering an apple.

"I won't eat that," I said, turning away, because she was a day too late to steal another two years.

"Wait, I know you," she called out, as I maneuvered down past an old hiker who whimpered as he gripped a cable. To ignore her was easy. I just focused on the joy the man's fear brought me. Not schadenfreude, but pleasure at the gulf between me and him. The whole way up, I hadn't wished to fall, nor had I anticipated falling, except during one little hiccup. "Let go and your body will balance with your mind," I said, startling the old man so much that I doubt I helped him. It was correct advice, though. I planned to follow it myself in the days to come, on all the new routes I was spotting, now that I was done running from what I loved.

GATEWAY TO THE OZARKS

BEFORE THE FIRST GENETIC clone of Thomas Jefferson turned thirteen, he would puzzle out the steps that had led to his conception, beginning with his mother Marissa's debt. To creditors the bipolar and unmedicated Marissa Barton owed fifty thousand dollars; to the drug dealers of Southwest Missouri, a smaller, more pressing sum. At Shoney's she had been earning two-fifteen an hour plus tips. When she signed up for the crack-cocaine study, it was for the cash, and after blowing through that easy money Marissa didn't balk at having her bills paid in return for submitting to a new kind of hysterectomy. Her daughters had moved out, her son was sixteen. If she wound up conceiving, said the researchers, she must carry to term or forfeit the payout. It made no sense, but Marissa was too strung out for questions and anyway, Bob, her boyfriend then, had had a vasectomy.

From an early age, Marissa's youngest child didn't mind spending time alone while his mother partied. Carl Barton's indoor pastimes—editing Wikipedia and drawing blueprints—were solitary ones. Compared to the mood elsewhere in his home, Carl enjoyed his bedroom and the quiet of his thoughts. He'd have explored the Ozark hills alone, too, but Silas Boyd Jr., the lisping boy across the road, trailed along chattering about *Warcraft*. It brought Silas no awe to discover an Osage arrowhead. If he mentioned school, it wasn't to wonder about a science lesson but to prattle on about the polyester pants their science teacher wore. Carl didn't care about pants. He edited encyclopedias. Lying beside Silas on the grassy hilltops, he would try to model the behavior of inquisitiveness, asking questions like, "Did you know these aren't mountains, but an eroded plateau?"

"You're an eroded plateau."

"Have you been to the Rockies?"

"Do what?"

"You take vacations?"

"My mom's a manager."

"Mine's a scientist."

"She's a crackhead."

"She studies stars."

"Want to get naked?"

"No," Carl said. The wind on his naked skin might feel magnificent, but what he sought climbing Thistle Mountain was serenity. Gazing into a wild but consistent landscape dotted with fiery blooms, he lay still.

"Maybe next time."

"Maybe," Carl said, and indeed next week Silas asked again. Again Carl said no. The third time, Silas proposed a game: they would drop their pants and kick each other in the balls, and whoever took the most kicks would win.

"I played it with my cousin and I beat him."

"Which means you lost."

"You're a dipshit," said Silas, which was outrageous.

"Fine, I'll do it, but with my clothes."

"Well, I'm taking mine off."

Silas let his pants fall. Proudly he stood there in briefs as Carl readied his leg and kicked, hard. The blow landed on target. Gripping himself, Silas lurched and leaned into the pain, trying not to wail.

It felt good to hurt someone as embarrassing as Silas. After a few moans, though, Silas stood upright again and grinned, which was when Carl fell forward into a fetal crouch of his own.

"You win," he howled in mock pain, upside down while Silas's pan-faced head moved closer. He shut his eyes. Was he okay? "I don't know," he whispered, wanting Silas to worry.

After a minute Carl opened his eyes to see Silas's crotch bulging out through his briefs. His balls appeared twice their former size.

"Did that happen when you played with your cousin?" Carl said, pointing.

Silas reached down to feel. "I might should put some ice on it."

They walked downhill. "Maybe a doctor, too," said Silas on the trail.

"One word to your folks, and I'll tell everyone."

"It doesn't hurt, it just chafes."

"Your balls grow as you get older," Carl said, more to reassure himself than to comfort Silas. "You're probably just growing up."

Back home, trying to edit, he kept losing himself in the same sentence on mountain formation. What was distracting him—his mother's snores? She slept through plenty of afternoons. The bills? His brother Frank was paying those. The pain he'd caused? Thinking about that, he pulsed with dread. He felt like a sick pervert. Out the window he noticed that the Boyds' car was gone. Where? The hospital. Why? His breath went shallow; he gulped down puke. Either

Silas had told, or he'd succumbed before naming Carl. If the latter, the exam would show a bruise or there would be no exam. If the latter again, no one had seen the kick or someone had, everyone had, and so on until Carl heard on the TV news that, in a freak accident, a local boy had suffered testicular trauma, gone into shock, and passed away on a gurney in the ER.

For days Carl waited for the cops to come for him and find his mother's drugs and arrest her too. He could warn Marissa to lie low, hide the pipes, but how to justify his concern? Better her in prison than him coming clean. On the fourth day he attended the funeral, so awful that he retained few memories of it later on Thistle Mountain's survey stone, eating wild berries until the knife-blade of dread chased him from his crime scene. A mother who paid attention might have connected Carl's behavior to Silas's death. One naïve question and Carl might have burst into blubbery tears, told all—it would have brought such relief—but the closest Marissa came was the day he found her on the couch, the curtains wide so any passerby could see her smoking.

"I'm studying Alberta," she said, when he went to shut them.

"What's Mrs. Boyd doing?"

"Gardening. Was Silas your best friend?"

"We knew each other."

"You were always climbing hills."

"I still climb hills."

"It's like, here I am, and Alberta's got energy for flowers? I never taught you about death. I've had friends die, but I wasn't young, I took you to that funeral and I . . ."

She trailed off. If she'd been clean, she might have felt in Carl's vacant shoulder-pat how anxious he had become.

"I know what death is," he said.

"Maybe sort of, but not really."

"Spot and Rex died."

"You remember Spot?"

"Mom, treat me like an adult?"

"Okay," Marissa said. Had Carl obeyed the moment's instinct, he'd have followed her gaze out to watch the Boyds' house like a film with her. Instead he returned to his room and drew plans for a four-story shopping mall. Sketching its soaring atrium, he was able to breathe easily. As he laid out a zoned city around the mall, a belief crept in that he'd intended to kill Silas, so he threw himself into a more ambitious project, a megalopolis made up solely of limited-access highways. In 2000:1 scale the cloverleaves metastasized onto page after new page, crowding out thoughts. Evolution, taunted Carl's mind in the distance, had paired Silas's instinct for being hurt with his for hurting. He only drew. Like editing, the work was endless. If he heard a car at the Boyds', he focused harder, and so on until August, when the principal began the welcome-back assembly with a moment of silence for their classmate who had tragically, et al.

Weighing the rhyming sounds of *silence* and *Silas,* Carl went hollow. Each school day would begin with a similar call for "a moment of silence for meditation or personal belief," and each day plainclothes cops would observe to see which kid froze up in guilt. Blueprints wouldn't help. Nothing would but some all-out war. Fort Leonard Wood was up the road. If China nuked that base, killing everyone, one boy's demise would come to seem a tiny thing. Their ballistic missiles had the range. *Atomic holocaust,* chanted Carl's wanting mind as other kids coaxed meaning from their friend's demise. "It's when you touch yourself too much." "It's AIDS." They seemed as excited as they were troubled.

Nodding to agree that such a death could claim no honest victim, Carl wiped out his school with hydrogen bombs, conveying to God what he wanted now that he'd given up on his mother.

In his first real memory, not a muddled glimpse but a sequence in time, Carl was four and Marissa was forty. They were eating popcorn on the carpet while reporters canoed through the Ninth Ward of New Orleans. He asked, "How far is that?" and Marissa replied, "Today? I need a place of peace. What's it called, Carl, when you can concentrate? I'm losing focus, you'd do better with your sisters, they'd cook you food, at least," and so on, patting his head to a peculiar rhythm. He asked no further questions. He was silenced by the thought that, even as he sat beside her, he might see his mother floating across the TV, face-down in the putrid waters spilling from Lake Pontchartrain. Lighting a pipe she'd never concealed from him, she said, "Don't tell," as if loyalty was something he still needed to learn. For years in his nightmares they'd been carting her off to jail. Those dreams stopped when Silas died.

Not that the death had coincided with an upturn in Marissa's life. Lately she was getting messed up with a taxidermist named Willy. One October night while Willy and Marissa were out joyriding, Carl tried to conjure another of the old dreams to prove that he still loved her. Over and over he crashed cars on dark highways in his mind until he was envisioning his own transfer from juvenile to adult prison, where the guard warned the other inmates, "This one's a sex offender."

He woke up gasping. Maybe you could dread just one thing at a time, he thought, walking to the kitchen to find Willy and his mother listening to Led Zeppelin.

"Past your whatchamacallit," said Marissa.

"Bedtime," said Willy.

"That's the ticket. We might go to the beach."

"Mom, did you ever want to be a scientist?" Carl asked, wondering whom she meant by *we*, and what beach. The Gulf was hundreds of miles away.

"I wanted to be a nurse."

"Cleaning up shit and vomit?" Willy said.

"Better than doing nothing all day," said Marissa, her first statement in a while that made Carl feel like they had something in common.

"Tell me about Bob," he said, naming his supposed father.

"Bob liked all those guys in the Highwaymen. Waylon and them. Born and raised in Texarkana and he drove an El Camino."

"Was he smart?"

"Same as anyone."

"Did he like science?"

"This is date night," said Willy, shifting Carl's mood. Frying fish sticks, he imagined again the fusion bombs falling, this time killing Marissa and Willy along with everybody else. He wished Marissa would clean up, climb mountains with him, enjoy the views, but it wasn't meant to be, and he'd learned to be okay with that; if she wound up in prison, he wouldn't go blubbering over it like he'd have done last year.

Carl dined in his bedroom with his blueprints laid out around him in a satisfying grid. Peering out at Willy's trailing headlights, he saw a shooting star, and read up on meteor showers. Already a fellow editor had written about the unusually dazzling outburst of 9 October. Tonight.

The Boyds' house loomed in shadow as he ventured into the chilly night. He lay down on the picnic table. Right away two meteors came dying across the sky. A boy who hadn't killed his neighbor might have relaxed into pondering the dynamical evolution of meteoroid streams, but Carl zeroed in on something else, the wishes you made on stars. I wish never to be caught, he decided as another one flared. These burning rocks weren't the bombs he'd asked for, but chances to remain free. I'm not a violent person, he whispered, as if that too was a wish. Don't send me to jail.

After a dozen selfish wishes he thought of wishing for Marissa to go clean, but she was under the sky; she could make wishes of her own.

Amid frog croaks like low-pitched roosters he heard his name spoken, and sat upright to face Silas's mom, Alberta Boyd, standing there in her Target shirt.

"It's the Draconids," he said, startled.

"You know, you look a lot like someone on TV."

Even in the dark Carl could see that Mrs. Boyd, with her sharp cheekbones high on a narrow face, appeared years younger than his haggard mother, yet he knew from Silas that this woman was the older one. "You've known me all my life."

"Not what I mean."

"My mom's away at the observatory."

"Have you made a wish?"

"I don't believe in that stuff," he said, coming around to what Mrs. Boyd might mean: she'd seen him on *America's Most Wanted*.

"Come talk to me sometime; I know your mom isn't as available as you'd like," she said, before walking away again.

More seething than afraid, Carl lay still in the dark. As a shooting star streaked toward a puny hill, he wondered if his father, too, had fallen politely quiet to mask rage. If he'd wished for nations' ruin merely to calm himself at insults to his mother.

The phone rang inside. It was his brother Frank. "Making a run down to Topeka."

"Mrs. Boyd was telling me I look like someone."

"Like me and the rest of us," Frank said, although they both knew Carl resembled none of the other Bartons. His chin was sharper, his eyes deeper, his voice reedier.

"Kansas is north."

"I know where Kansas is."

"You go up to it, not down."

"Does Mom want her usual?"

"Did Bob have more kids?"

"Weird thing about Bob, he'd had a vasectomy."

"So it can come undone?" Carl asked, feeling like he was learning that his whole life had been a dream.

"Mom was being evicted, is why I did my first deal. Except she had more cards than I could cover."

Frank paused. Carl heard clicks of interference. Not just a dream, he thought, but some nightmare, where the terrible truth lurked invisibly around the bend.

"I found this place called Consumer Credit Counseling. Drove back home with the brochure, and Mom told me, I've paid my debts. Then nine months later. Anyway, her usual?"

Was Frank punking him? Was he strung out? A vasectomy reversal, the encyclopedia said, cost thousands of dollars. Marissa fretted over sums as small as twenty dollars. Maybe she'd blackmailed a rich guy. Carl went to her bedroom and pulled out a box from under her bed. It held disability applications, credit card statements listing hundred-dollar cash advances, and a crayon drawing of mother and son on a raft in the Ninth Ward, storm clouds swirling above. He tore it down the middle. Burn the box and the house too, he was thinking when he came upon a letter from a man named Jim Smith, at a place in Virginia called JCP, dated 2000.

Congratulations on your acceptance, it read. *Peruse the guidelines, sign the confirmation and liability form, and return them before*

*April 1. Upon receipt, our office will contact you about travel. If you
have questions, call us at (703) 921-2258.*

There were no guidelines, no letterhead, only this page whose
number gave a busy-circuits signal when Carl called. He'd been
born ten months after 1 April 2000. Pinching his arm, he tried to
quell a sense that something demonic had occurred. A thin orange
line glowed in the east. *Civil twilight,* he read, *begins when the geo-
metric center of the sun is six degrees below* . . .

The phone rang. I've solved it, he thought, they're calling to
congratulate me.

"Ms. Barton?" said a woman.

"I'm Mr. Barton," Carl said.

"Is Marissa Barton your wife?"

"Marissa is my mother."

"Then give me your dad."

"I'm searching for my dad."

"Well, go find him," said the voice, at which point it became
clear this was the police, letting Carl know—as he intuited before
he heard another word—that he wouldn't be asking Marissa about
the letter, now that she and Willy and two of their friends had
driven off a cliff en route home from date night.

There were so many kinds of bombs. Fission and fusion weap-
ons, split into subcategories that ran to thousands of words each.
Delivery systems, trajectory phases, navigational equations; still,
some missiles lacked pages of their own. Across the wall from his
grieving sisters Carl opened the Article Wizard to channel knowledge from schematic to encyclopedia. Hour by hour the templates
grew. Propellant, warhead, blast yield, launch platform. There
wasn't some high heaven where Silas floated over to Marissa to whisper why he'd died; the dead quit knowing you, so he launched a new

attack, not some vague bomb batch anymore but Dong Feng 31s and Julang-2s carrying payloads of ninety-kiloton MIRVs. From Jin-class submarines they flew toward America. The impact was cataclysmic. Instantaneously there was no crime scene, no Ozarks, no Bartons, only a lurching sensation like what he'd felt before the car wreck, a cold shiver, an extraneous coincidence, rather than the souls of the newly dead passing through him toward their starting place.

The bungalow Carl's brother Frank shared with his wife and their young sons sat on a four-lane bypass by a check-cashing store. There was a billboard tower in the front yard, and no internet except at the library in a nearby flat town. Once a week Carl could use his sister Sheila's computer to look up Jim Smiths who led to various dead ends, but he couldn't live with his sisters because of their jealous boyfriends. At his new school the top student, Wade Jones, had recently died in a wreck of his own. Since Carl was smart, the other kids pegged him as Wade's replacement, conflating Wade's and Marissa's wrecks the way Carl conflated Wade and Silas. Every mention of Wade returned Carl to a familiar sick place. He began to worry also about the bad education he was receiving. In the work of some of his Wikipedia colleagues, he could perceive the gap between autodidacts and the classically educated. While his mind recalled numbers and diagrams well, and he saw beauty in symmetries both natural and syntactic, he knew next to nothing about the arts. He spoke one language. Rich kids on the coasts were vaulting hopelessly ahead while he lived on some highway. One Friday he sneaked out of school and biked across town to the Montessori academy to tell the director, "I'm Carl Barton. I want to enroll."

"Your parents should come fill out an application."

"My mom died, and I don't have a dad. I live with my brother."

The man's tightening smile revealed the essence of what he would say: parental involvement was part of the pedagogy, and it wasn't cheap; there were no scholarships. Rather than beg abjectly to mop floors, clean toilets, Carl thanked him and left. Riding home, he despised his sisters for attracting bullies, his brother for being a criminal, their mom for raising such a sorry lot. He delivered that anger into his pedal strokes. When he crossed the edge of a plateau into a rare descent, he was already soaring. Then it was like he'd leapt into another biome: sky crisp against a long prairie, exhilaration pumping out of his heart. His T-shirt an airfoil, he stood upright in perfectly dry air. The sky's crispness, he thought, derives from aridity. When places looked pretty on TV, it was because they weren't humid. For the first time since Silas had died, Carl felt hopeful. Screw the Ozarks. There were better mountains, and he could go climb them and ride down and his sorrow would be his own fault—that's what he was thinking when his tire blew and he went tumbling over the guardrail.

For a few months his hard luck multiplied. His blueprints disappeared out of his old house. A time-share developer bought Thistle Mountain and the hills around it. He learned that from his sister-in-law, Denise, as she fed and bathed him. Laid up all day with his broken legs propped up on the coffee table, he found that asking for help made him feel worthless and ashamed. Under his stinking casts his little cousins crawled, singing "London Bridge" while he sketched buildings and requested meals of minimal complexity, prepackaged things he hated the taste of, until one morning his brother and sister-in-law were arrested.

It was a lot like the old dreams: six cops busted in, handcuffed Frank and Denise, read charges of interstate drug trafficking, and carted them off. The social worker who stayed insulted

Carl with children's books and cartoons. Still, he continued to dismiss as magical thinking the notion that he had hurt the Bartons with his warheads, until the boyfriend of his sister Becky, who was preparing to take him in, stabbed Becky in the heart.

His sister Wilma wheeled him to Becky's funeral, where his sister Sheila arrived with a black eye. "What's with your eye?" asked Wilma afterward.

"It's been a tricky week."

"I'm on probation, so he can't stay with me."

"I can't keep him myself."

"Have you heard of Jim Smith?" Carl asked his sisters.

"I ain't good with names," Wilma said.

"Mom's files say he admitted her to a program in Virginia."

"That box went to the landfill."

"Did she mention Jim Smith to you?"

"Did she talk to any of us about anything ever?" said Sheila, with a tinge of lament that made Carl sorry for her. Imagining the childhood they'd have shared if she'd been younger, he wanted to ask, Do you think we've endured an unlikely amount of suffering? She would only have answered that God gives no more than you can take. He kept mum. His hapless sisters seemed apart from him, logic problems to puzzle out rather than humans to love.

They moved Carl into Sheila's apartment in the gaudy tourist town of Branson, next door to a country music theater where Sheila's stalker worked at the bar. To take out a restraining order would get Glenn fired, so Sheila didn't. "While I'm at work, don't answer the phone or the door," she said before leaving Carl alone to repair his reputation as an editor.

On her computer he abridged and amended page after page that he'd thought of as his to administer: the St. Francois Mountains; the Boston Mountains; the Salem and Springfield

Plateaus. Together these made up the Ozarks, whose stems occupied Carl for days. The Ozark Mountain forest ecoregion; ecoregions in general; biomes; then back in toward the specific, updating citations, testing links. It wasn't always intellectually valuable work, but it was satisfying, necessary work. Thousands of others were doing it at the same time. To imagine them all gardening their plots of knowledge together, fertilizing soil, plucking out weeds, gave Carl the well-being he used to find outdoors.

"Shouldn't you go to school?" Sheila asked.

"Mom enrolled me online," he lied. "The work's electronic." It was true he listened to Open Yale Courses while sifting through search results for all three-word combinations in his mother's letter. Some work took place offline, like when he phoned the sperm banks of Virginia and every company called JCP, saying things like "I need to talk to Jim Smith," and "This is Marissa Barton, calling about my account." No one knew a thing. It seemed he would never learn why he stood apart from his relatives. By the time he happened to turn on the *Late Show*, on the evening of the day when one cast was removed and he graduated to crutches, he was ready to give up.

The guests, said the announcer, included a Marin County boy named Heath Nabors IV, "who, after comparing the DNA of humpback whales, songbirds, and humans, alleges to have isolated genes for musical ability." That boy strolled onstage and the TV became a mirror. It was Carl's doppelgänger, with his same oblong jaw, his fair face, his gangly arms, his questioning eyes, his age and stature.

Grinning in a way Carl had never seen himself grin, Heath Nabors IV sat down on a couch. "Your parents must be proud," the host said.

"I've been emancipated from my parents," Heath explained,

with brash pride that sent Carl reeling into self-loathing even as he sat transfixed.

"At the age of eleven?"

"I'm twelve," Heath said. Carl saw how he must have been sticking his own chest out. Giddy, he heard only little phrases of Heath's. "Tonal metaphors." "Acoustic exhaustion." He imagined such a boastful voice booming out of himself while he kicked Silas, and here was how his lip must twist up in pride before bragging: "My dad made a deal. If I can play every instrument in the orchestra by sixteen, he'll buy me a Ferrari."

Heath produced a flute and whistled a display of his technical mastery. Whatever the fourth Heath Nabors had been emancipated from, the third was missing a boy, thought Carl as his sister Sheila entered the room.

"Has anyone knocked?"

"Does Heath Nabors IV ring a bell?"

"This kid? Is he famous?"

"Look at him," Carl said. His twin was explaining his goal to decode whale speech; Heath doubted that birds had much to say.

"I saw this episode a while back," Sheila said, as if to prove once and for all that Carl's smarts derived from his paternal line. "He resembles you a bit."

She walked away. How could she not see it? Because of studio makeup, Carl thought. Because of schooling: i.e., money. Because of dread, the absence of it in Heath's face, the presence of it in his own. A widening gap, already manifest. The adult Heath would be handsome like film stars, while Carl would be a worn and hard Ozark man.

A new kind of dread pooled like mercury under Carl's skin as he glimpsed a life almost lived, an injustice so common to fairy tales.

He dialed long distance information to ask for Heath Nabors. Soon he was writing down the number for his identical wunderkind's father. He held his breath and called it. When a woman answered, he asked for Heath the Fourth's number. She gave it to Carl. He keyed it in. After two rings, he heard a click.

"Yep?" said his own impossible voice, and then Carl could have wept, because it was as if he'd tapped into some plane where Marissa was alive, where she had sought treatment, where she had put Carl in music camp instead of letting him wander to maim and kill.

"I saw you on TV just now and I'm—"

"Another one?" said his ostensible twin, without surprise.

"We're identical. I can prove it."

"No shit, moron. A musician recognizes the register of his own voice, even if you do sound like a hick."

"What did you mean, 'Another one?'"

"Do you love architecture and have a genius IQ?"

"Why; do you?"

"I asked you, shit-for-brains."

"Have you been spying on me?"

"I'm sure we have cameras behind our eyes."

Carl twisted the blinds shut, shuddering to think there could be film of his assault on Silas. "How'd you learn about me?"

"By answering the phone, numbskull. You're the fourth to contact me. We're all clones of Thomas Jefferson."

In six keystrokes Carl had conjured an image of the man whose glinting eyes, high cheeks, and laconic smile could have belonged to an age-progressed image of himself. It seemed preposterous, and he knew that it must be true.

"Father of liberty," added Heath, in case Carl hadn't read that part of the encyclopedia.

"How'd you figure it out?"

"I'm a geneticist."

"You're twelve," he said, even as he read that there'd been calls to exhume Jefferson and test his DNA for paternity of the Hemings children.

"At our age, the original Jefferson spoke Latin, Greek, and French."

"Who else knows? Your folks?"

"Only the other four."

"So they're studying us from somewhere."

"Didn't I say so, dipshit?"

Carl was getting tired of being called stupid. Although he hadn't injured Heath, or done anything in Heath's presence to be ashamed of, he wished for the Tsar Bomba to detonate over Heath's house.

"What did your folks do to you?"

"I guess you could say my folks loved me too much. But look, gotta go. Let's talk tomorrow. There'll be a Skype conference at noon."

It was like Heath expected Carl to simply intuit how to find him online. And maybe, by virtue of his genes, Carl should be able to. If Heath was telling the truth, Carl should be able to command, to enslave, to speak with eloquence. Having cross-referenced the Jefferson page, he knew his abilities. He could foment revolutions. An orphan of radical inclinations, he recalled a quote from the man about refreshing liberty's tree with the blood of patriots. Human blood, Jefferson had said, was liberty's natural manure.

Carl relaxed into a sense of rightness. "Okay," he said, "let's talk then."

"Well, that's dumb of you," said Heath, "since we haven't even traded handles."

To avoid notice as identical genius quadruplets, the clones had been using Heath's blog as a private social network. "Try to catch up" was the last thing Heath said on the phone, and Carl spent an hour doing that, tracing his way through threads about language coaches, soccer camp, vacations abroad. Luc lived in Grosse Pointe, Talbot in Alexandria, Mason in Park Slope. Luc had had extra pages stapled into his passport. It grew tedious to read about the boys' academic prowess, their overbearing fathers, the careers of their mothers. One mom was an Assistant Secretary of State, the others a producer, a renowned scholar, and a surgeon. Pondering what to tell them about the Bartons, Carl clenched up. It was wrong to feel ashamed of Marissa for being dead; still, however he felt about any subject, his clones stood a good chance of feeling the same. Astronomer, he practiced saying. Researched astrobiology. Lived in Biosphere 2.

He learned that Jefferson had loved botany and agriculture, philosophy and exploration, classical ratios, that his curiosity had been ardent about all subjects but geology. Carl had enjoyed learning about the Ozarks' billion-year erosion. If I like geology, he thought, I'm an improvement on the original. To read the Virginia Statute for Religious Freedom gave him chills. It had gratified his shy, intense, soft-spoken, humble forebear to gaze beyond hills toward the vanishing point, as Carl did now in Branson, thinking, This is who I am. Perplexing though it was for the scientists to have given Carl to the Bartons, he thrilled to anticipate what was in store at noon. We'll be farmed out to lead revolutions, he thought. No, they'll put us through Harvard. We'll be the founders of a Mars colony.

All night Carl read about the American Enlightenment. When the sun rose over Lake Taneycomo, he set his alarm for 11:30 and tried to sleep. Across the wall he could hear his sister quarreling with her boyfriend. The gist was that Sheila was a slutty whore and the boyfriend was done with her. "I love you," she repeated as Carl imagined his sister alone, wrapping a Christmas present to herself after he abandoned her for his real family. Was he willing? What value to intelligence if it didn't help his loved ones? Wasn't it his job to make things better?

No, exhaustion was driving his mind to melodrama. The Bartons hadn't bothered with Christmas in years.

When at last he slept, he dreamt his mother was a stock car driver with cancer, wired up to the transmission of her Chevrolet SS. She had to drive fast enough for the alkylating agents to be released. Her pedal was to the floor, but it wasn't enough, and by the time the alarm sounded at 11:30 the cancer had spread to her brain.

He got up and ate cereal, reading the news. A Nobel laureate in economics had passed away. After he updated the man's page with the date and cause of death, he clicked through the prior awardees, back to Frédéric Passy, French economist and first peace laureate. The man had been born in 1822, when Jefferson was seventy-nine. If Carl made note of the linkage, which existed only in the form of his thoughts, it would be deleted. To change *Passy* to *Pussy*, *economist* to *dipshit*, would get him exiled as a vandal. As if that mattered, he thought, feeling less and less like himself, until noon, when he clicked in to a video discussion in four little squares that each held his moving face.

"I'm Carl Barton," he said, gulping down an impulse to run from this horror show of lookalikes with raised cheekbones, yellow-brown curls, and eyes of false beseeching kindness.

"No shit," said the one with a cello propped up behind him. Heath.

"Say your name again," said the boy in the lower right.

"Carl Barton," said Carl.

They all hooted with delight. "Do they have electricity where you live?" drawled one, in mimicry of an accent Carl had never noticed in himself.

"I'm on a computer," he said, to more laughter.

"Where'd you grow up, on a train?"

"We moved around for my mom's job," he said, uneasy. There was no parallel between the other boys' mockery and the Jeffersonian qualities—politeness, curiosity, decorum—that he'd lain awake reading about.

"Did she drive a truck?"

"She studied the night sky."

"In the Ozarks?"

"The Ozarks have night sky."

"What did you score on the SAT?"

"I'm twelve."

"So am I, but I faked an application to Harvard to see if I'd get in."

"We have to attend different schools. Luc has dibs on Harvard, I've got Princeton, Talbot Yale, Mason Stanford."

"So no one else knows?" Carl asked, but Heath was talking over him: "Hold your computer up and spin it around."

"It's a desktop computer."

"Point it out your window. Is that the projects?"

"This is Branson. There's no projects."

"You know how science works; every experiment needs a control group and a white-trash welfare group. We hypothesized your existence weeks ago."

Carl had always been different from the people around him, but not because of money. At his school most kids had been poor. He hadn't felt ashamed. He tried laughing along with the others, and it seemed to work; the teasing bounced back toward Mason.

Mason had been caught making his dog suck his cock; now he had to go see a psychiatrist. Talbot guessed they were all genetically inclined to do the same. If so, the clones must have wished for bombs to fall on their cities, too. Heath, Talbot, Mason, Luc, or anyone would have kicked Silas to death.

Carl wanted to confess his apocalyptic fantasies, but the boys had shifted to wondering whether DHS had noticed their similar passport photos.

The debate, neither scientific nor analytical, bounced meaninglessly back and forth. Hadn't; had; couldn't have; must have. Even the speculation—"They'll learn soon"—was perfunctory and incurious.

"Are any of you religious?" asked Carl, trying to think like a scientist.

"Duh, Ozarks, religious wackos don't do in vitro."

"If none of us are, it's a noteworthy finding."

"Read the blog," said Luc, a reply Carl heard again every time he tried steering the talk away from matters of insignificance. The inanity of TV plots; the clones' annoyance at camp humor. Though he agreed, he took no comfort in shared opinions on trivial matters, unless the others were hiding crimes like his and their curiosity was buried alongside their darkest shame. It was important to bide his time. If he said suddenly, "Last year I kicked a boy and he died," he would be labeling them all potential killers. They might clam up, cast him out. So he only said "Me too" in response to shared taste after shared taste: elegant designs, anthemic rock chords, Tuscany. To be poor was to know less. "I loved it there," he said.

After the call ended and the chat continued by IM, they bragged in foreign languages about their prowess in those languages. Carl used Google Translate to reply. Mason asked about his investment portfolio, and he culled an answer. It wasn't just fear of being exposed in those lies that unnerved him when they scheduled another dialogue for that night. In some odd way he was beginning to feel proud of his family. No, he was troubled at a deeper level. He didn't think the scientists could have deliberately ruined the Bartons' lives, nor did he believe they could have peered into the boys' future and pegged his as the most doomed. Still, it would have been nice to speak to inquisitive people about these ideas.

It had been too long since his last blueprint. He spent the afternoon drawing a federal center to house four coequal chambers of an imaginary government. When it began to resemble a honeycomb, he considered modeling the power structure on the colonial nests of bees. That didn't suggest a way forward. The chambers, he decided, would be analogous to the human heart's. A chamber to give oxygen, a chamber to take it back. A chamber to receive blood, a chamber to return it. White blood cells to fight off contagion, kidneys to remove waste, all controlled by the brain, and the honeycomb he revised into the Great Sphinx, jutting into the ocean on a craggy cape. When the government body was done, he hobbled down Branson's gaudy main drag toward shapely green hills beyond. Another week and he would be hiking again. Did the others spend time outdoors? They skied and sailed, but if they yearned for wilderness, they hid it.

At the turn for Silver Dollar City, Carl considered visiting that old-timey park, finding out if its log flumes and gold-panning stations would awaken latent genetic memories, but he had no money. While Heath and company reaped the advantages of their geography and wealth, he couldn't even enter Silver Dollar City.

Was his circumstance a maze to puzzle his way out of, he

wondered, sulking onward? Was his bar set lower; must the others graduate summa cum laude from Oxford to match a middle-school dropout's escape from the Ozarks?

The woman who spoke his name seemed to be hovering suddenly behind Carl's head. He pivoted with his crutch to see an SUV driven by Silas's mother, Alberta Boyd.

"Carl, is that really you?" said Mrs. Boyd, pulling onto the shoulder. "What on earth did you do to your leg?"

"I was exploring."

"Silas is at Randy Travis. I'll give you a ride!"

Seized by eerie panic, he knew she must have deduced the truth—*we all have cameras behind our eyes*—but then he recalled that Silas had been a Junior, named for his father.

"Thank you, ma'am. I like to walk."

"You must live with Sheila. Does she still sing?"

"She waitresses at a theater."

"That's nice." He had never heard his sister sing. In silence he and Mrs. Boyd faced each other. Come talk to me, she'd said, with no idea what she was urging. He'd grown furious because it would have felt so good. Even now, light-headed, holding onto her sideview mirror, he nearly sobbed at the idea of it. Of admitting anything. The bombs, the crack, the other clones, the blueprints, so many secrets, amassing until a dam burst.

"I kicked Silas in the balls," he said. "He died because of me."

"That's sweet of you," said Mrs. Boyd without even blinking, "but it was his pervert cousin up in Tulsa."

Over, he almost said. You went over to Tulsa, not up.

"I'm not a pervert, but he asked me to do it and I did."

"He admired you, Carl. You were a good friend."

"At first I wouldn't. I didn't think I'd like it."

"It was his cousin Rabbit. He's in juvie now, up in Tulsa."

Why wasn't he glad? Would he feel this way forever? Trust me, he wanted to shout. He didn't. Again she offered a ride. "Walking clears my head," he said, refusing again, so Alberta Boyd drove off, leaving him alone with the old dread, fierce as ever, haunting him like a real ghost, and not even Marissa's; where was her ghost? Hadn't Carl done something bad to Marissa, too?

There were motels, family fun centers, a wax museum with a parking-lot carnival where he played midway games, tossing darts at balloons until he won a stuffed black bear that wore a toddler-size Branson T-shirt. *Gateway to the Ozarks*, it read. He wedged the bear in his armpit as a pad for his crutch. Back home, in wait for his pseudo-brothers to come online, he pulled up the Branson page. "Branson is a city in Stone and Taney Counties in the US state of Missouri," it began.

Placing the cursor after the subject of that sentence, Carl added, "known as the Gateway to the Ozarks," setting off the new text with commas since it was a nonessential clause.

He clicked through to his hometown's page: a stub, in danger of deletion. He wrote about cash crops and commerce and linked to similar text in stubs about other Ozark towns. He was hoping to save them. There was still time. He edited mountains nearby, mountains in other states, other countries, even other worlds. With his atlas open to the moon he searched for peaks unnamed, as if he possessed any worthwhile knowledge of them. He gave Mons Moro a page. He gave a page to Mons Gruithuisen Delta. Like his description of Branson, they would be removed for lack of significance, but he denoted elevation and coordinates and name origins until the bell chimed.

"Hey," he said when the other clones came onscreen, expectant, peaceful, mischievous, resourceful: four kinds of happiness to contrast his empty dread.

"Hey, you still sound like a hick," Heath said.

"You're still a fuckwad," Carl said, and the others laughed in good spirits, seeming glad he'd joined in.

"I was reading about dialect discrimination. Apparently, it's bigoted to make fun of hillbillies and hicks."

They chuckled as if they knew what was coming. Even in his unease, Carl wondered if Heath's upbringing stifled his innate polite humility, or had history failed to catch that Heath's was the more natural Jeffersonian mode?

"What's that say behind you?" asked Luc, of the stuffed bear.

"I won it at the fair."

"Branson, then something smaller."

"Gateway to the Ozarks."

"You're the gateway to the Ozarks," said Heath, resurrecting Silas's last living taunt: "*You're* an eroded plateau." The words echoed off Thistle Mountain and across the months and miles. To take the clones' laughter to heart was ridiculous. Obviously Carl wasn't an eroded plateau. By the joke's mechanics, whatever he uttered was rendered absurd. Was it so absurd, though, to call a reborn Enlightenment naturalist who climbed hills and studied maps—who turned the local range's name over in mind until it struck him as some ur-language's first word—the gateway to those mountains?

They were still laughing. He had had enough. Every day he'd been soaking in shame, until he was wishing for the world's end. Not just over Silas. His mother; his sisters; strangers' pity at those wretched funerals. His petty edits to the encyclopedia—garnish, not knowledge—and on a mountain, when someone had asked did he want to undress in the hot wind, he'd said, "No." If the geneticists were rooting for the underdog, they'd tensed up while he talked to Mrs. Boyd, and now they would clench their teeth again to hear Carl say, with no motive beyond catharsis, "I killed a boy last year."

Immediately he had the clones' attention. "There was no one else for miles," he said. "It was a warm summer day, and Silas took off his clothes, because he wanted to play a game."

Listening, each boy exhibited his own tic—Luc's slanted smile; Heath's twitching eyelid—but they were genetic equals, whose reactions must mean the same thing: they were all struggling to admit to wrongs on par with Carl's crime.

Of course, he thought. Look who they were copied from! They had the DNA of a man who'd confined his boy slaves to a nailery under threat of the lash. Ones who fought were sold into the Deep South. Children as young as ten, living on a mountain at the edge of wilderness, but in a cage, hammering out ten thousand nails per day. Tranquility was the apotheosis, Jefferson had written. Freedom from worry; freedom from pain. Ataraxia and aponia: the Epicurean ideal. Would you spend your life harping on freedom from worry if you were free?

No, thought Carl, as he described tricking Silas out of kicking back, the terrible hike home, the news, the funeral, the aftermath. "Maybe that's why I've learned no other languages," he said.

Heath was typing. Another boy murmured. Carl waited for text to appear.

"Sounds like you needed that off your chest," said Luc.

Or was it Mason, or Talbot? Both were suppressing the same smirk, as if no one else had anything to get off his chest. No words had arrived on Carl's screen. "Look at the depraved things Jefferson did," he said—an accusation, like saying, Look at the depraved things *you've* done. Look at the freakish secrets plaguing you! They wouldn't look. Like their progenitor, they'd been raised too properly to defy the convention against reticence. That much was apparent to Carl now that he'd confessed. Not confessing had been miserable. Physical violence led to emotional violence, as it had done for the founders, so corroded by the guilt of enslaving that they'd dreamt of epochal ruin.

"No, you're the depraved one," Heath said. "Except for being genius polymaths, the rest of us are normal."

"Maybe you're right. Maybe my mom tainted my DNA when she smoked crack."

He was beginning to hear the twang in his accent. He muted the speakers, not in spite. He had quit wishing for bombs to obliterate his twins' cities. Suddenly the illogic of absolving himself by means of more harm seemed as obvious as his origins. Their lives were gaming out a wager whose odds had been set before Carl was born. Clone X to exceed historical Jefferson's capabilities. Clone Y to prove capable of same as original. Clone Z to fail. If Heath and the rest kept up their tepid investigation, they would decipher a scheme to use settings of disparate privilege to pursue a trite inquiry into nurture and nature. Unplugging his modem, Carl forsook that quest for lack of significance. There were more intriguing questions. His injuries to the Hemings family alone had had Jefferson stoking the Reign of Terror. Whether or not that aligned with the record, Carl's own thoughts proved it. He had worthwhile knowledge that would rewrite history. His dread was going to change the past. Not long ago, when he was still devoting his considerable brainpower to cluster-bombing, the ones who'd bet against him must have believed they were sitting pretty.

CULT HEROES

IN NOVEMBER 1995, on the eve of the federal shutdown, the high-school mountain biking champion of California set off down the Central Valley to look for his father. A Fresno Superior Court judge was demanding both parents' signatures before she would approve Hunter's emancipation petition. Unless Hunter found Arthur Flynn at a Flagstaff address from years ago, his mother would have to testify at a public hearing. It was a glorious fall day, the hills crisply amber against a mackerel sky. His friend Cody had come along on the promise of a ride. Both boys raced as expert juniors; both were skipping school.

"Thank God your mom's crazy and your dad vanished," Cody said near Bakersfield, "or we'd be in chemistry."

Hunter forced a laugh even as he cringed to hear his mother described that way. She was devout, not crazy. Since her car wreck she'd been paying sixty dollars an hour—from Hunter's race winnings—to a Christian Science practitioner who prayed with her for the pain to end. Lately those injuries had segued into something more deep-seated. After she tithed the entire purse from Hunter's win in Tahoe, Cody had convinced him to cut her off. "Do it before you get sponsored," he'd said after *Bike Magazine* labeled Hunter "the likeliest Jordan of our incipient sport." In the inaugural run of the Leadville 100, Hunter had placed in the top ten overall, including adults. His nickname since then was Death Wish. Kids broke bones on those steep, rocky trails where winners topped forty mph. Worried parents sidelined many a natural talent, but to Emily Flynn, asking her son to slow down was like telling God she didn't believe in him. Velocity was a beguiling illusion meant to test their faith, which explained why Emily at the time of impact hadn't been wearing a seatbelt.

East of Mojave the valley gave way to brown desert lined with ranch trails that Hunter gazed at longingly from the wheel. Lately he'd been staring at singletrack and doubletrack the way other kids looked at porn; something welled up in him until he needed to touch it, feel it under him. "Look," he said to Cody, who glanced up from examining the road atlas.

"We'll be like fifty miles from the Grand Canyon," Cody said.

"Let's drive up and see it."

"No, let's ride to the bottom of it."

"It's a national park. They'd arrest us."

"Which is fucking dumb."

"The trails are kind of narrow," said Hunter, picturing hikers leaping to their deaths as he and Cody raged down a precarious path.

"It's probably a fifty-dollar fine."

"It's more if you kill someone."

"Or if you get a yeast infection from rubbing your pussy on the seat."

"What?" said Hunter.

"Medical bills and all."

"I'm just saying it's narrow trails."

"Then let's hit Moab and ride Slickrock."

"Okay," Hunter said, liking that plan better. He was still adjusting to his coming freedom. After the emancipation, he would drop out of high school and buy an RV that he and Cody would drive to race after race, detouring whenever they felt like it to Slickrock's petrified dunes or any trail in America. He'd been telling Cody it sounded awesome, and it did, except when he imagined his mother living alone.

There was the practitioner, of course. Recently Joseph had offered to hold Emily's hand as she walked away from Error back into Mind. God helped people ready to render themselves fools in the eyes of others, Joseph had said, and Emily need only look to her sister— Hunter's aunt Amy, who'd died of the flu—to see what became of fear. Hunter couldn't tell whether the man was a grifter. Maybe Joseph was in love with Emily, as she seemed to be with him. Hunter imagined his concern was only a conjurer's trick, as Emily would say about the sky shimmering above Barstow.

In the Rodman Mountains a butte with steep zigzagging paths mesmerized Hunter into drifting onto the rumble strips. When Cody snapped alert, Hunter pointed to the blunt hillock. The sun was sinking behind low mountains, causing the shadow line to retreat up the butte.

"We can beat it," he said, pulling off.

Without even closing the van doors they rode three minutes flat to the base of the rise. Hoisting their bikes over their shoulders, they scrambled up a scree field. The light was withdrawing. In a skidding rush they raced the sun until the gradient eased and they could mount their bikes again, slicing their way up to the summit in time for another sunset.

"Fucking A," said Hunter on that high dais, wishing he could pause time.

"What a beautiful painting God has made for us today," Cody said, mocking Hunter's mother again.

"It *is* beautiful," Hunter might have replied, but that wasn't part of the deal of Cody's friendship. Nor could he agree aloud that the sight hardly seemed real.

"Race you to the bottom," he said instead.

"First let's admire God's handiwork for a few minutes."

He laid his bike down. As soon as he turned to face the radiant show of orange light, Cody leapt on his own bike and went screaming down the butte's north face.

Hunter gave chase. It felt incredible to charge downhill. He rode headlong onto a jutting boulder that launched him out over Cody, through the air. He landed diagonal to the grade, skidding hard right. From behind him he heard Cody cursing, but just for show. A good race was what Cody had wanted, and Hunter, who liked to please people, was giving it to him. He bunny-hopped gully after gully. Feeling serene, he kept a lead all the way back to the van, where his worry resumed over his father.

Hunter retained no memories of Arthur Flynn beyond his mother's few stories, which all took place during his infancy. According to Emily, Arthur had suggested putting Hunter up for adoption because of the shape of his head. "I've got a conehead for a kid," he'd told every nurse at the hospital, irked in a manner that seemed jokey until he phoned Catholic Charities and arranged for a Sister Bernice to come by. A far-fetched tale, but could Emily have cooked up such a particular account of drenching the nun with a pitcher of sweet tea? Or Arthur's last words to her, "Keep your napkin in your lap," or the strange gifts he'd sent from the

Arizona address: lingerie two sizes too small, a family-sized box of Crystal Light?

Driving east, Hunter rehearsed not mentioning those things to his father. Unless Arthur Flynn looked thrilled to see him, Hunter would ignore his face, demeanor, everything except his signature on a form.

In Flagstaff, after checking into a Motel 6, the boys drove to 310 Beaver Street to find an empty house with an auction notice posted in front. Hardly had Hunter registered relief before Cody said, "This blows," so loudly that a neighbor heard.

"If it's Buck you want," said that woman from her porch, "find him at Charlie's Bar on the main drag."

They thanked her, drove away. "Should we try it?" Cody asked.

"I doubt Buck's Arthur," Hunter said.

"Hunter, on that piece-of-shit bike of yours, you're a badass, but off of it you're a festering pussy."

"Okay, Cody."

"Did you hear about the girl in New Mexico?"

He shook his head. He knew Cody was about to describe yet another victim of Christian Science.

"Her parents let her bleed to death. State took them to trial, but the court ruled in favor of religious freedom."

Over the past few months, since the pedal incident, Cody had been telling Hunter about similar kids in practically every state.

"That's a tragedy," Hunter said.

"Could happen to you."

"I'm not a hemophiliac."

"It's a cult like the Branch Davidians."

"You're right," he said, in order to stop talking about it. He had a disquieting thought. His bike, a Cannondale Killer V 900, was hardly a piece of shit. Still, it paled beside the Litespeed Cody had stolen after giving a fake ID to test-ride it. Although Cody's anesthesiologist father could afford any bike Cody believed he deserved, Cody had told his parents off and they weren't speaking anymore. Now he sought for Hunter to ditch his own mother, too, so that Hunter's winnings could fund their racing life.

"This feels like something I should do myself," he said to his friend. "Maybe you could go back and plan tomorrow's ride?"

"It's true a pussy wouldn't plan as hard a ride as I will," Cody said, and did a three-point turn back toward the motel.

Alone, Hunter crossed town to a strip mall laid out below the moon-lit mountains he would explore tomorrow. Facing the pink neon of Charlie's Bar he sat there arguing with himself. Head back now, he thought, and lie that Buck looked nothing like him, wasn't even white. Emancipation had been Cody's idea, not his. But to picture that Christian Science con man whispering away his mother's pain sent Hunter trudging into the bar's dim interior, the papers folded into his training journal.

He laid the book down on the bar. Above him hung the Arizona state flag and a rainbow flag, flanked by elk heads. Upbeat country was playing loud.

"Rum and Coke," he told the bartender.

"How about just a Coke," was the reply.

"I'm being emancipated from my family," he said, taking a seat in a row of plaid-shirted men who were hunched over their drinks.

"Let's see some ID."

"It's at home."

"Maybe a Sprite."

"Forget it," said Hunter, as a ruggedly handsome fellow a few stools down seemed to take notice. He looked about fifty, with sandy hair and a sharp jaw like Hunter's, and they both watched the bartender pour the Coke.

Hunter felt himself being observed. He took the drink and sipped, refusing to stare back. Eventually the man beside him left, and the sandy-haired guy scooted over onto that seat.

"Ain't seen you here," he said to Hunter.

"I don't live here."

"Name's Buck."

"Okay," Hunter said, nervous.

"You like it?"

"The bar?"

"My name."

"I guess so."

"Most twinks do."

"Most what do?"

"How about you?"

"How about me?"

"What's your name?"

"Hunter," he said.

"That's cool. Hunter and Buck."

"What did it mean, 'Most twinks do'?"

"Sounds macho, and so does yours."

So Buck was talking about their names. With a shrug Hunter feigned indifference. The truth was he despised his name. For a year now, he'd been a vegetarian. The kids in his class who hunted were the ones who said cycling was for fags. Hunters struck Hunter as cruel, callow people. When his parents had named him Hunter, they had misread him in a manner he could cite in the court petition.

"Let me guess why you're in town. To hike the canyon."

"I'm a mountain biker."

"Ride the canyon."

"Against the law."

"Government's shutting down."

"Huh?" He wondered if Buck was a cop.

"Budget crisis. At midnight tonight every government employee's being furloughed, thanks to Slick Willie."

"Are you sure?" Hunter said, imagining himself and Cody becoming history's first riders of the Grand Canyon.

"That includes park rangers."

"But it's still illegal."

"I'll take you."

"We've got a car."

"Who's we?"

"Me and my friend."

"So you've got a friend."

"Are you surprised?"

"You two want company?"

"Not especially."

"Pick cotton, and it's time to look for snakes."

That sounded like nonsense, of a piece with the lingerie and the Crystal Light. Then Hunter spotted two men holding hands by the wall.

"I know who you remind me of," Buck said.

"Who?" Hunter shut his eyes to brace himself for the shame that he and Buck would both feel if Buck turned out to be the man. He isn't, Hunter told himself. Wrong name, wrong face, wrong everything.

He opened his eyes to find that Buck's dumbfounded expression hadn't changed.

"It was up in Kalispell, Montana. Middle of winter, blizzard conditions, but we figured out how to stay warm."

"How old was he?"

"About like you."

"Is this how you picked him up, too?"

"Honestly, I doubt I had to try as hard."

Hunter glanced at the form sticking out of his journal. All he needed was a signature. Whoever Buck was, he would probably forge one in return for a kiss or something. They could even laugh together about Hunter's thinking Buck was his dad, Hunter was telling himself when he heard, "Case you change your mind," and saw Buck slip him a business card that read *Arthur Flynn, National Park Service Ranger.*

He stopped breathing. "What's with your finger?" Buck said, because Hunter's right ring finger was dangling limply as he picked up the card.

"Cycling injury."

"Well, call me," Buck said, and then he walked in back.

Sensing scrutiny from all sides, Hunter stopped breathing. Did all the men want him? Or were they laughing at his stupid hope that Buck would be worth talking to? The air thinned, the walls closed in. It was like his mother's Lord was doubling down on the illusion, pressing his face into it, a face he wished to inspect for similarities to Buck's. Did the sickle curve in Buck's jawline resemble Hunter's, now that he'd chiseled himself down to competition weight? Girls at school had started whispering about him, which had given him a shivery thrill. Now he only felt sick.

He laid two dollars on the bar. Back in the parking lot he called his mother collect from a pay phone. He'd lied that there was a bike race, and now he told Emily he and Cody had tied for second place. "Some twerp from Utah beat us. How are you feeling?"

"Better now that Joseph is here," she said.

"Isn't it kind of late?"

"He's been worried about me." She sounded warmed by the idea. "It's more than just the wreck; there's something else."

"The prize was a thousand bucks," he said, to test her reaction.

"Will you and Cody split it?"

"We each get our own."

"Congratulations," she said again, too neutrally to indicate much. Did she know about the petition somehow? He'd been hoping not to tell her about the proceeding until it was over. To obtain her signature, he'd disguised the form as a permission slip for a race.

"In the morning we're riding our bikes down the Grand Canyon," he said.

"That sounds beautiful. But be careful."

"We'll wear our seatbelts," Hunter said, and then quickly hung up, feeling mean for making fun of her like that.

Was Cody rubbing off on him, he wondered, driving back to the motel? What had come over him? Did he believe it had been Emily's idea for Buck to flirt with him at a bar? She could have warned him; she must have known Hunter would go looking someday. She could have argued for a different name. He turned Pearl Jam up loud. Trying to feel better, he drummed all his fingers but one to the beat. His right ring finger drooped lifelessly against the wheel, same as every day since the evening when he'd swapped out his toe clips for clipless pedals. He'd been waiting for Cody to come ride. Tugging with a wrench, he couldn't get the pedal axle to budge. He grabbed the opposite crank, pulled hard. When the axle finally gave, the force slammed his hand down onto a chain tooth.

The metal cut straight through to white bone. Hunter fainted at the sight. When he came to, his mother was kneeling beside him, applying pressure to staunch blood that wasn't real. It was a test of their faith, and it lasted until Cody showed up and drove Hunter to the hospital.

"Are you totally insane?" he said on the drive.

"I hardly feel it," Hunter replied, still woozy.

The ER doctor, who said Hunter had sliced his tendon in two, sewed the wound up and referred him to an orthopedic clinic. By the time that office opened, Hunter still hadn't asked for his mother's consent for surgery. You couldn't be made of matter if you reflected God's nature. Afraid the question would erect a wall between them, he let it go. The tendon retreated up his arm, or appeared to, and his finger dangled limply from then on.

"Talk to him?" said Cody, back at the Motel 6.

Hunter held up his journal as if it contained the signature.

"Sweet. What's Pussy Senior like?"

"Kind of fat," said Hunter, knowing how quickly Cody lost interest in people who weren't in riding shape.

"That's lame. I found us a sick ride."

"I found a sicker one," said Hunter, piquing Cody's curiosity. Where? Who'd told him? His dad? Some wino? A pro cyclist visiting the Center for High Altitude Training? Juli Furtado? Tinker Juarez? Hunter refused to answer until the eleven o'clock news, which confirmed that the US government had suspended its operations, and the entire park system was closed indefinitely to both visitors and rangers.

All the way up US 180, over blasting Metallica, Cody shouted into the predawn dark that they would be devirginizing the canyon. Not until they veered around the shut gate through a stand of pinyon pines did he quiet the music and fall silent as if in uncharacteristic reverence. A glorious sunrise was igniting the canyon prongs. "It's surreal," Hunter said, full of a strange unease, as if his mother was right, and his survival on the ride down depended on faith that the land was make-believe.

"Yes, another lovely painting this morning," Cody said. He was masking his awe, thought Hunter. He didn't want to admit that the world could seem too beautiful to be real.

"Think we'll be arrested?" Hunter asked in the empty trailhead lot, pouring water into his bottles.

"Everest used to be off limits to climbers, too."

"Is that a no?"

"It angered the gods. I say fuck that."

He almost wished Cody would fear arrest, so he could pull out Buck's card and say, Here's how I know we're safe. If he mentioned Buck out of context, it would seem like he needed to talk about him.

A solitary hawk was circling as they aired up their tires. They loaded their saddlebags. Hunter led the way into a stand of cliffrose. The leaves of those twisty trees pricked him and made him shiver in the warm air. He wheelied over a fallen pine. Barely had he landed again before the world fell out from under him and he was soaring downhill, almost too fast to control.

To keep from flying over the bars, he hung back with his weight behind the saddle. The path narrowed to the width of his tires. Before him gaped miles of empty space. He leaned hard left. Over the wind Cody's screams sounded like thrill-cries, changing in intensity so many times that Hunter paused at a wide place in the trail in case it meant something sinister.

Straddling his bike, he counted mesas that rose between him and the snowy North Rim. All part of the illusion, he was musing when Cody came careening around a bend. He skidded halfway to a halt before knocking Hunter over.

"What the fuck?" Cody said, as Hunter untangled himself from his bike.

"You screamed like you were in trouble."

"You were winning again, dickface."

"I'm only riding," he said.

"Quarter mile ahead without trying."

Cody was right, Hunter hadn't been trying. "Go in front then."

"No, Death Wish, you'd be riding my ass."

Cody wasn't smiling. "I don't have a death wish," Hunter said, startled to realize his friend's attitude wasn't just a shtick.

"Well, I do. I'd rather die than lose to you again."

"I didn't realize we were racing," he lied.

"Last night on that butte, middle of nowhere and you still wouldn't let me win. You flew right over my head."

"I'm sorry," Hunter said, honestly surprised.

"'I didn't realize we were racing,'" Cody repeated in an effeminate whine. "Like mother, like daughter."

"What's that mean?"

"You think you win races because it's not real. It's all your fantasy, and in your head you deserve to be champion."

"Fine, I deserve it," Hunter heard himself say, as his fondness for his friend dissipated into the enormous emptiness.

"Let's find out," said Cody, pushing his way between Hunter and the cliff edge.

After Cody had vanished around a bend, Hunter stood there in a daze, straddling his bike. Emily was sick at home, thinking kind thoughts, while healthy Cody was here living out his hateful dream.

If I'm winning because I believe I ought to, then I'll fucking win, Hunter thought in belated reply as he pushed off downhill.

He pedaled with all his might. One inch to the right as he accelerated, and he would be dead. One inch left, and he would ricochet off the cliff wall into the open air. But he was in control. He shifted to the smallest rear cog. To lean into curves was exhilarating. His whole body hovered over the chasm. He fell into a trance, exulted, breathed, put his life at risk too many times to count, until his hands were numb from the bumps and the trail petered out by a boathouse on the shore of the Colorado River.

He laid his bike on the gravel beach and stood in awe of the colored canyon wall that rose before him. Except for the rippling water, it was quiet. His thoughts about Cody seemed small to him now. No longer caring who had won, he looked toward the boathouse. Cody must be in there, intending to scare him. Let him have his moment to gloat, Hunter thought, walking over. When he shouted Cody's name, it echoed back. He arrived at the wooden structure, reached for the door handle. As he did, the door swung wide. "Boo," he cried out, producing a gasp from a uniformed female ranger.

She dropped the kayak she was dragging. "Help," Hunter heard himself say as she touched a gun in its holster. Pretend to need water. I've wandered for days. But she noticed his bike and moved her hand onto her radio.

"Are you dumb or insane?" was her first question of many. Had he thought about the hikers he might have killed? Imagined that the rangers would vanish at midnight? Had he ridden helmetless in a show of bravado, or had his helmet fallen into the canyon, as he so easily could have done too? Was he aware of the laws she was citing in a rush? No, he indicated with a head shake to each rhetorical question, he wasn't, hadn't, didn't, and so on until she asked for his friend's last name.

"I'm here alone," he said, hoping Cody could see what was going on.

"I scared you more than you scared me," the ranger said, and then she radioed to headquarters.

"Is his bike expensive?" asked a man over the radio.

"Kid, how much did that bike cost?" she said.

"I'm not hurting anyone," Hunter protested, wishing Cody were here after all. Cody could say, "Know who we are, bitch?" and take off running, whereas Hunter felt knee-jerk guilt to think of this woman as a bitch.

She detached his front wheel and chained it up with the kay-aks. "See you up top," she said, and told her colleague to meet Hunter at the trailhead.

"I want my wheel back," he said meekly, scared for his friend, even as he feared Cody could overhear him being a pussy.

"You can hike out with the rest of it, or I'll keep the whole thing."

The ranger escorted him over to where the bike lay. He dragged it out of her sight behind a stand of mahogany, where he sat down to wait for Cody.

The sun was high overhead now. He grew thirsty and uncomfortable. Half an hour passed by. He wanted his wheel back. The ranger hadn't even asked how it felt to ride the canyon. Did she not wonder? Was it a thrill she couldn't begin to imagine? If Cody would just show up, they could mock her incuriosity together, but it was becoming difficult to believe his friend was okay.

He looked up at the terraced cliff. If he'd been guiding events by religious conviction, Cody would signal from above with a pebble. There was only the wind in the trees, the flow of the river.

When he couldn't sit still for the disquiet he felt, he balanced the bike on its wheel, held its handlebars at chest level, and pushed it in front of him.

It was hotter than it had been. He drank some water. By the first switchback his arms already ached from their outstretched position. He moved his right hand to the saddle. His limp finger bounced with every bump. Occasionally in dust or manure he could make out a scant set of tire treads. This didn't mean Cody hadn't ridden past, only that on such a skinny trail their paths had overlapped.

He inched uphill, scared to have rounded such impossible bends. The trail never remained straight for more than a few feet. At one point where the route veered acutely left, he couldn't see how he'd made it past without dismounting, unless the canyon was an illusion after all. Nor did he recall this particular arrangement of spires whose crows cawed as if to say, *Getting warmer*.

He scrolled through his odometer to find that his maximum speed had been an unimaginable twenty-nine miles per hour.

He'd ridden downhill in closeted superstition and survived, but Cody had ridden an atheist and now lay dying.

To shout Cody's name brought only his own voice echoing in ever fainter reply. He shifted positions and walked in front of his bike, pulling it like a plow. He drank the last of his water. Scenes played out in his mind of finding Cody at the trailhead, screaming at him about this dirty trick. He teared up to imagine the sheer relief. He pictured the ranger at the morgue, saying to Cody's desolate parents, "If only your son's friend had admitted that he was down there."

If she hadn't stolen his wheel, he would ride back down and change his story, have her radio in for help. It's that bitch's fault, he was telling himself when he spotted a second set of treads.

Heart racing, Hunter propped his bike up against some sage-brush and followed the tracks to where they trailed away at a shale slab.

A few feet farther, two sets picked up again, but of course below here he'd retraced his path and there would need to be three sets.

It was time to pray. I'm sorry for being unkind, he chanted in mind, trudging uphill again. If his mother wished for Christian Science treatment, she could have it. His lack of empathy had killed Cody. Be generous, and the universe repaid you. He vowed to call from the first pay phone and drop his emancipation suit. He was responsible for his own acts and felt ashamed of them all. Fall in love with the world, and you quit trusting in God to guide you through it. I trust, he chanted, I don't love the world, until he rounded the final bend to face a uniformed Buck, arms crossed, asking, "You and your friend like the ride?"

Back when Hunter was friendless, before Cody first lent him a spare bike, there'd been nothing but TV. He'd gotten to be well-versed in the tropes of drama, such as the hurt son who abhorred his dead-beat dad. On TV some teenage boy was always shouting "You ruined my life!" to a father he barely knew. "How dare you show your face here?" Hunter didn't wish to be a kid like that. What if Emily had lied, and the tea and lingerie had come from another man? What if Buck didn't know he had a son? Tempting as it was to bellow curses, Buck might not grasp their meaning, in which case Hunter would feel ashamed for years to come. Too thirsty to speak anyway, he walked past, to the van. He opened the cooler. Only when cold water had flooded the dry cavities in him did he consider how sug-gestively Buck had enunciated *friend*.

"My friend's gone and I can't find him," said Hunter, his voice cracking enough that something changed in Buck.

"What's his name?" Buck said, seeming to have detected at last that Hunter was only a boy who needed help.

"Cody Avery. It's been hours."

Buck walked out of hearing range and spoke on the radio. When he was done, he told Hunter, "Seems you're under arrest, but hang tight."

Hunter sat on a log and flipped through old issues of *Bike*. After a while a helicopter flew overhead and vanished below the canyon rim. He didn't want to think about what that meant. Staring down at the glossy trail photos, he focused on keeping Cody's obituary out of next month's issue, occupying himself with that hope or prayer until Buck ambled over to ask what he'd been doing in Charlie's Bar.

"I drove past and saw it."

"So you're twenty-one?"

"Thought maybe they'd serve me."

"How old's your friend?" said Buck, again adding a subtly lascivious innuendo to the word *friend*.

"We were both born in seventy-eight," Hunter replied. His stomach growled audibly. He felt a swell of something, roiling him more than hunger.

"There's a steakhouse past the boundary."

"What?" he said, as if Buck had delivered a non sequitur.

"Show up with me, they'll serve you drinks."

"I already ate," he said, certain now Cody was observing from the afterlife, snickering in derision.

Buck held up a key chain with a pink rabbit's foot. "Your friend will be okay," he said, rubbing it.

"Do you believe in that?" Hunter said. He heard the latent anger in his own words. On the verge of losing control, he counted the seconds, timing his breath.

"No, you're just cuter when you smile."

Hunter pulled out his training journal. Although he no longer desired emancipation—felt petty to have considered it—he handed Buck the court papers.

Buck pulled out reading glasses, read down the first page. "I see," he murmured.

"Do you see?" said Hunter.

"I believe I do."

"What, exactly?"

"That finger, for one."

Hunter had to look down at his hand before he understood what Buck meant.

"You know, your church founder paid dentists to fix her teeth."

"Medicine back then was hardly better than praying," Hunter answered, startled to hear himself defending Emily's ideas.

"She wrote that it was a still birth."

"It wasn't," was all he could reply.

"Well, is there something to write with?"

How dare you, Hunter almost said now, just like those hackneyed boys on TV—you ruined my life—but he only shook his head.

"Your ma's the superstitious one," Buck said. "She wanted a baby in seventy-seven because it's a lucky number. I skedaddled. See you in seventy-eight, I told her."

He was stroking his rabbit's foot again. Hunter shut his eyes. Earlier in his count he'd reached seven; now he whispered eight Mississippi, nine Mississippi, ten.

"Know what else? My dad had a stroke, and Emily took my hands and said, 'Arthur, this life is but a stem on a rose.'"

"A thorn," Hunter corrected. Eternity lasted forever, while life was but a thorn on a stem in a garden of flowers, all manner of them, all colors, fertilized by the divine, infinite mind.

"Thorns grow on stems, last I checked. Is there really no pen?"

In the silence, as Hunter's glands prepared spit for a fit of rage, he could hear Emily's soft voice describing those flowers. He got ready to drown her out. "Never show your face again!" would be his first words, and then he would lose track, screaming anything, because of course there were pens. He'd been called out in a silly lie; Buck could see them in the coin tray, the ones Cody had used to denote bike routes.

"They're out of ink," he whispered.

"Can't sign without one."

"I don't need your signature anymore."

"You're not under arrest. Jenny wants me to call the state police, but I'm the one told you to come."

"As if I care," Hunter managed to say. He no longer wanted to stifle his screams. To do so dishonored his mother. Still, that was the effect of Buck's lines: he breathed more slowly again, peering into the future at the end product of rage. Buck, already a sad sack, now KO'd into suicide by this kid he might have loved if given a chance. Whom he hadn't meant to hurt—and so forth in a maelstrom of empathy run amok.

"Speaking of calls," he said, "I should alert Cody's folks."

"There's a phone at the entrance kiosk. Anyone asks, say Buck Flynn sent you."

Hunter climbed in the van. "Be right back," he said, disgusted by how he'd suppressed his emotions. Throttling even apt rage was what made him a pussy. He drove away. He bypassed the shut park gate without stopping. After a while he passed a Western Sizzler that stood alone on that red plain. There was a pay phone. He sped up, took off his seatbelt. "I'm an atheist," he said aloud as a tractor-trailer rushed toward him, straddling the yellow line and shaking the van in its rough wake.

Someone braver would have to call Cody's folks, he was thinking when he spotted a shirtless cyclist coasting toward him down the center line. A jersey, red like Cody's and rippling in the wind, hung out of that rider's shorts.

Hardly had Hunter stopped the van before he was rushing out onto the empty highway, catching a bewildered Cody in his arms.

"Dude, chill out," Cody said.

"You're alive," Hunter choked.

"Yeah, shit was sick. I almost died so many times. Are you...?" He didn't need to say *crying*, now that the answer was obvious.

"I waited forever."

"Must have made a wrong turn; I'm the one who waited."

"There weren't turns."

Cody opened the hatchback door to load his bike. "What the hell?" he said.

"They confiscated my wheel. They're looking for us now."

"Rangers? No way. That's awesome."

"I thought you were dead."

"Yeah, you wish. Ready to go?"

"Go where?" He was weeping openly now under that endless sky. He could see forever, and there was nowhere he wanted to go besides home.

"What time did you reach the river?"

"I didn't notice," he lied.

"Bullshit. I was 8:21 and ten seconds."

"You probably beat me," Hunter said—another lie. Not that it mattered if they'd descended different routes, but he recalled touching the water at 8:18.

"Damn straight," Cody said, launching into an account of the hairy turns and narrow ledges. Hunter winced to hear of every skid, as if the telling put him in danger again. "How about you? You crash?"

"Only when you hit me."

"We'll be cult heroes. We'll name our RV *Cult Hero*."

"You be the hero. I need to focus on my mom."

"Let's try not to be retarded, okay?"

"I think something's really wrong with her."

"Yeah, Death Wish, it's called her brain?"

"I'm glad you're not dead," Hunter blurted, suddenly needing his friend to speak sincerely too. To be reverent for a moment, like at sunrise; to ease up so Hunter could admit it all felt like a magic trick, this crimson desert whose deadly cliffs he'd navigated by force of will. He'd stopped trusting in reality. There was no helicopter. If it were out searching, wouldn't they be hurrying up the highway, deeper into the red dream of earth? He yearned to come clean, and then for Cody to admit he believed in something too. Whatever that thing was, it had held Cody in its stead down the canyon, or Cody had perished and been resurrected by Hunter's wishes—but Cody said only, "Guess I'll emancipate myself from my own parents. Christ."

They didn't stop being friends. Hunter just spent more and more time by himself, riding Squaw's Leap alone at night, racing downhill by moonlight and imagining himself not as a bike champion but as someone girls could enjoy being with. He was toned from riding; Buck had liked him. Thinking the acute empathy that had crippled him in Arizona might work to his advantage, he tried to cultivate a look of innocent serenity so that girls would take him for a Buddhist or an abuse victim. He even got a little turned on to think of himself this way, or at least he did until his mother grew sicker, with abdominal pain that the practitioner blamed on malicious animal magnetism.

It was good he hadn't gone through with the emancipation, Hunter realized after Emily ran out of money and Joseph stopped coming around. He dropped out of races to stay home with her. He refused interviews that Cody granted. The cult hero prediction was coming to pass; everyone from *Bike* to local rags in the mountain towns wrote up their adventure. All the publicity seemed to improve Cody's riding. He placed at the nationals and got sponsored by Trek and Powerade. The following month he called Hunter to say, "My name's in this issue twice. Yours, once."

"Congratulations, Cody."

"Congratulations and . . . ?"

"I'm happy for you."

"No, get jealous or something."

"But I'm not," said Hunter, wishing it were a lie, wishing he still cared to compete.

"Try not being jealous when my emancipation goes through."

"I'll be glad for you if it's what you want."

"Fuck you in the pussy, Death Wish."

There was one thing Hunter did envy of Cody's: his healthy family. Cody's parents might live fifty more years. Unless she switched religions, Emily didn't have much longer. It wasn't hard to guess what was wrong. Yellow eyes, itchy palms, no appetite. He wanted to shout at her as angrily as he could have screamed at Buck. Tell her she was a moron to give up for nothing; cry out that she was stealing herself from him. Was it because she was a coward about doctors? Or was she only scared that Matter wasn't Error, and there would be no God, no heaven, no illusion, nothing but herself and Hunter, watching TV in their split-level by the Yosemite Freeway? He wished to berate her until she gave in to his greater will. She nibbled at food he prepared for her.

One day near the end, she held his hands and said, "Sorry I'm keeping you from your races," and he mumbled, "I'm sorry too." Two seconds hadn't passed before he was rebuking himself again. Sorry for what? Sacrificing himself? Wishing his way toward this circumstance? He had chosen it; somewhere north of Flagstaff his beliefs had taken a wrong turn and here he was, but she wasn't paying attention. Her eyes had shut. I've been emancipated, he thought, although technically speaking she lived on until he reached the age of majority.

THE GNAT LINE

THE NEW LAW, WHICH BARRED registered offenders from living within one-fifth of a mile from a school, church, or other place where children might congregate, had drawn circles onto the Georgia map in the tens of thousands. In the mountains and cotton country the circles stood alone, but Atlanta's overlapped in cascades and formed tiny islands shaped like boomerangs, narrowed to inches or confined to commuter lots and the inner lanes of I-75. The nearest viable parcel lay north of Acworth, where the terrain grew steeper and a power cut climbed up a bluff from Lake Allatoona. There, among tents in a hilltop copse, lived five rapists, one attempted rapist, and a man convicted of indecent exposure. All were white. The youngest was twenty-five, the oldest fifty-four. On Mondays a truck delivered water coolers to an office park down Glade Road; Gus, the first settler, would steal a few to hang from trees as showers. He drove a MARTA bus, and Bruce edited at CNN. Jeremy worked at the World of Coke. Patrick clerked at the

Flying J station. Travis mopped floors at Boeing. Allen sold cars. As for the exhibitionist, he had been a personal injury lawyer.

2.

Stephen had been a partner at a respectable firm downtown until one morning in 2007 when he brewed coffee in the nude as a school bus stopped outside his townhouse. There were cellphone photos of him by the wide-open front window, empty coffee pot in hand. One mother claimed that he must have planned it that way: "Don't you brew coffee in your kitchen? Where the coffee pot plugs in?" Although the judge handed down a suspended sentence, the registry meant eviction from Midtown. When he showed up at camp, the others wondered if he was hiding a worse crime—"Exposure? Lame," they said—but he didn't care what monsters thought. He spent days in his new office and evenings in his tent, reading. He did nothing else. In October he read the last three volumes of Proust; in November, much of Thomas Hardy. Thanks to the court-ordered drug tests, he could focus again.

One night after a rain, Bruce, the stout video editor who was always grinning, stuck his head into Stephen's tent and said, "Which ones you done with?"

"Which European modernists?"

"For the fire," Bruce said, climbing through the half-open zipper to kneel by a stack of tomes. "*The Magic Mountain. The Man Without Qualities.*"

"Touch one and I'll shoot you."

"How can you not have qualities?" Bruce continued down the row. "*The Naked and the Dead.* That's your memoir, I guess. Who's the dead?"

From his legal briefcase Stephen pulled out the S&W Model 625 he'd carried since law school without ever firing. "No trespassing."

"Felons can't own firearms."

He aimed the revolver. "Planning to go tell?"

"Fine, keep your books, crazy. Guess there won't be a fire."

"I guess not." If he'd never hit it off with his neighbors at the townhouse, he wouldn't make friends here. The camp wasn't permanent, not for Stephen. Once things died down, he would get his name expunged. Meanwhile he kept his distance, worked long hours in his new office in the strip mall, dined alone in bars, read himself to sleep, until the night the temperature fell to fifteen.

He lay alone shivering for hours before Gus, the buck-toothed, scrawny driver, called, "We know you're up."

Wrapped in his sleeping bag, Stephen walked out and took a seat at the fire. Bruce passed the vodka. Stephen drank and listened to a debate about Michael Vick, the quarterback charged with running a dog-fighting ring.

"Asshole should rot in jail and never play," Gus said, staring at the glowing end of the branch he held. "This was our year."

"Naw, Falcons don't got a year," Bruce said.

"Law should keep him a fifth-mile from vets and pet stores."

"In college," said Allen, the salesman, "I intercepted his touchdown pass."

"Could you get him free?" asked Jeremy, a blonde kid cute enough that Stephen sometimes forgot to ignore him along with the others.

"I couldn't get myself free," Stephen said, glad for the excuse to stare. It wasn't just that Jeremy was cute; he seemed a reasonable human being. There were three tiers: the ones like him and

Jeremy who'd been criminally maligned; the ones like Patrick who belonged in the camp; and the rest, who should never have been paroled.

"So you defended yourself?"

"Not the best idea," Stephen admitted. The other partners had been shunning him by then. "Judge disliked me."

"Vick's judge hates Vick," Jeremy said. His blonde beard stubble glowed in the firelight, tempting Stephen to touch it. "You eat meat?"

"Cooking some?" He wondered if they were progressing toward something.

"No. They do worse to pigs than dogs. I say lock up pig farmers, let Vick go."

"I hope he comes and lives here after parole," Gus said.

Allen shook his head. "The blacks have got their own camp, across town."

Watching his frosty breath mingle with the smoke, Stephen wondered if his neighbors were joking. Didn't they realize that Vick, after serving his time, could live where he pleased? He supposed he didn't care. Embers rose into a starless sky and he wished a winter storm would bear down, trapping him at work to save him from a night here, but there wasn't one snowflake, and by next day's close of business he was choosing a recovery meeting from the list to fulfill his weekly mandate.

"My name's Pam, and I'm a sex addict," said a woman with vibrantly black curls, across the circle from Stephen in the church gym. "Over time I lost interest in dealings that didn't involve sex. My family, even my dear kitty-cats bored me." The group thanked her. The vaguer a story, the more likely its teller had come for a signed note. Vera was taking it day by day; Blake was trying not to play games. Churches didn't have gyms, Stephen decided. It was a former school, a place twice forbidden, so that he imagined a double gnat line surrounding it. That was his name for the circles ordaining where he could and couldn't live. The real gnat line ran horizontally across the state, near Macon. "Folks is different below it," Patrick had said, but the only difference was the gnat problem.

Stephen wasn't listening. Clockwise around the circle he studied faces: a dead ringer for Lee Harvey Oswald, an exterminator in a pink tie, and then none other than Jeremy, the cute one from camp, in his World of Coke shirt.

"I'm Jeremy," Jeremy said, his glazed eyes staring at the one called Vera, "and I'm addicted to booze, sex, various drugs. Down in Savannah when I was in high school, this fellow Kevin smashes into my mom. He doesn't have insurance, so he begs her not to report it, he'll pay cash. Mom agrees, but her back starts to hurt. Pretty soon she's walking stooped over. Three weeks later, Kevin hasn't paid a cent, her car won't run, pain gets worse, she's a hunchback by the time I go to Kevin's."

Jeremy swallowed and took a breath. "Kevin tells me his dad just died and he'll pay next Friday. Okay, but I see this brand-new electric guitar in his back seat. Another week. Mom's in agony. I drive back and damned if Kevin's car hasn't been fixed up like new. So I bang on the door and this kid wearing Mickey Mouse ears peeks through the blinds."

As soon as Stephen heard *Mickey Mouse ears*, he knew Jeremy wasn't speaking as himself, but as Bruce, the wisecracking video editor from camp.

"Door's hollow. I bust through. Kid runs to his room. Next thing, he's got this cigarette lighter and he's burning my arm. That was what flipped the switch. I grab it and burn him back and say okay, here's what's coming."

Stephen shifted in his seat. He knew what was coming. Having researched his neighbors on LexisNexis, he couldn't listen, but he couldn't block out the words. *Please*, he wanted to scream. Maybe Jeremy heard him somehow in his mind, because he turned and noticed Stephen.

He paused his story. "I can't sit here and nod," said a guy in Army camouflage.

"We'd like you to leave," Vera said, folding her hands.

"First I need a form signed," Jeremy said.

"Actually I'll be the one leaving," said the Army guy, and he did, followed by two women. It seemed like the group might break apart, until Stephen heard himself speak his own name.

"I used to get shitfaced and invite guys over," he said, feeling the tension begin to resolve around him and in his own shoulders. "Anyone willing to come. If I had a partner, I cheated. If he said no don't, you're the one I love, I dumped him. The only ones I wanted to stay were trying to escape, like my last boyfriend, this kid from NA whose arms bent way back like Gumby. He was trying to quit. I did everything in my power to keep him high so we could just fuck fuck fuck fuck until he leapt off Stone Mountain."

With thirty curious, supportive eyes on him, Stephen paused. What came after Seamus died? The bus. He wasn't about to tell that part. He mumbled a few words about living with the pain. The room thanked him. Jeremy in particular should be grateful, he thought, for how he'd redirected their energy—except from all the histories at the camp Jeremy had chosen Bruce's. The self-calumny was baffling. *In sobriety, we found we know how to instinctively handle situations that used to baffle us.* Did Jeremy believe Stephen had invaded his meeting? He could be a loose cannon—a convicted sex offender, after all. Maybe Stephen was in danger. As the circle's testimonies continued, his anxious mind drowned them out.

By the end, he felt keyed up enough to rush to the guy in the pink tie, get his form signed ahead of Pam and Blake, and hit the road before anyone could speak his name.

3.

Like his neighbor in the woods, Jeremy visited no meeting twice. Like Stephen again he lay in wait for winter storms. It was a matter of aesthetic taste, the snow, and so was Jeremy's behavior in the meetings, where no member had the right to stand in judgment, where most appeared as smugly pleased in their neutrality as the Honorable Diane Stokes had been at Jeremy's sentencing. To put their objectivity to the test and then watch it evaporate satisfied him. He'd portrayed Bruce several times, honed the performance until it marshaled a real oppressive energy that peaked at the Unitarian church, where he might have emptied the gym if Stephen hadn't destroyed the moment.

The sex rooms had few locations, so Jeremy often wound up at the more populous groups, as well as Crystal Meth Anonymous, Pills Anonymous, even Survivors of Incest Anonymous, channeling voices like Travis's, the janitor who'd earned his living selling rohypnol that his brother smuggled in. Had he drugged girls himself? Travis said no, while Jeremy's answer changed with the rooms' moods. He tended to give his own name. If need be, he assigned himself an addiction to match the group, but his story's spine was Travis's roofies, Bruce's boy, Allen's girls, Patrick's dancer, Gus's gang bangs.

"I'm an addict," he told an unusually diverse group at the Triangle Club the evening before the snow. "Growing up in Hiwassee, my cousin Garth and I were racing to see who'd get laid most. Same girl twice didn't count, you had to get new girls. It's a small town. Ladies got wind. Nothing we did up there was a crime, though; all Hiwassee could do was chase us down to Clayton."

He kept ramping it up. They would hate him no matter what. They wanted him ashamed of loving Melissa, and if he could learn to feel shame over that, it might be a step toward turning the love into something else. Something positive. He had petitioned to move to Alaska, where it was dark all winter and snowed in July and he'd heard there were twelve men per woman. Of course his mother didn't want him to go. The snow he awoke to on 1 December felt like a premonition to ignore her.

Five minutes down the slippery trail, ten to de-ice his windshield, twenty to creep toward I-75. An hour later, when he arrived downtown, inches of snow lay unblemished on the empty parking lot of the World of Coke, closed due to weather.

He walked six deserted blocks to a diner, where he bought the paper. Emotionlessly he read about the presidential primary. He'd backed away from caring about stuff like that. His candidates, like his teams, lost every time. That was the kind of guy he was. Most people had bad and good luck mixed together, but not Jeremy. He'd been accepted to Emory by accident, a mistake the school had cleared up weeks later. There was a fifty-fifty chance he had the Huntington's gene. When he was ten, his class had flown to D.C., and he was the only boy without a window seat on either flight leg.

"You'll get stranded," said a waitress, slightly pretty, her hair the color they called dishwater. She had no supposed neutrality to put to a test; still, folks all reacted one way or the other, and Jeremy liked to know where he stood.

"Is there a school or church nearby?"

"Doubt it. We're downtown. Why?"

"I'm twenty-five, my ex is twenty-two, and it was seven years ago."

She tapped at her order pad as if waiting for the point.

"Have you heard of the Georgia Sex Offender Law?"

"Oh, okay," she said.

"When Melissa's dad found out, she was applying to this summer program at the University of Seville. He decided I must have brainwashed her into going there, because you know what Spain's age of consent is?"

The waitress shook her head. "Thirteen," Jeremy said, not to prove a point but to state a fact. If she thought he meant that it sounded nice, that age, she could join the queue. He paid and left. Walking on, he luxuriated in the cold. Drifts on the east side of the street came as high as his knees.

At Turner Field his mother phoned. "Jeremy, are you inside?"

"I'm at work in a warm building."

"You'll catch cold."

"No smoke breaks, remember? I quit."

"I'm immunocompromised, you know."

"I know," he said, lying down in the parking lot where the old stadium had been. His bed could be the former home plate, where Deion Sanders had once stood and batted a foul into Jeremy's glove, back when his dad took him to games. Holding the phone steady with his shoulder, he moved his arms to make angel wings.

"Will you come by later to feed the birds?"

"If the weather lets up," he replied. He lay under a soothingly gray sky, musing on Alaska. Talkeetna, to be specific. In a cold place people would know who he was. Men in Georgia looked at him and saw someone who wanted to sweat in Spain. Heat speeded up neurodegeneration, probably. It made cops restless. One sweltering June day a cop had asked if Jeremy wanted a Taser up his ass. Police in Talkeetna would be calmer, he thought, closing his eyes. For most people there was bad and good luck, mixed together, and he let himself hope his was just a longer pendulum, ready to swing back to carry him north on a surge of fortune. Sleep would test it. Freeze, or wake up in a white room with a nurse leaning in, and no guard hovering. "Nothing wrong with you except your mind," she would say, and he would ask, "You mean the snow?" hoping for once somebody didn't know.

As soon as he had shut his eyes, a policeman pulled up and offered to help.

"If you're not a dick, don't be a cop," Jeremy said, and then of course he was raising his empty hands, getting patted down, explaining why he'd paused to rest and why his address was a public tract in Bartow County.

The cop relaxed. "Case you're wondering," he told Jeremy, "it shows on my screen what you did."

"I wasn't wondering."

"I mean, my wife was sixteen when we first hooked up."

"Mary was fourteen when she had Jesus," Jeremy said, because the day a Georgia cop helped him would be the day he died.

"Does Acworth know about you all?"

"When it gets warm, those guys like to come play their games."

"Doubt it helps, talking to them like that."

"You're right, Officer, I'll try being nice."

"I'll give you some advice. A week or so, they're gonna come shut that place down. You'd do well to have a new residence lined up."

"Police put us there to start with."

"The papers have found out. Sheriff got them to sit on their story until you guys are staying someplace safe."

"Gee, thanks."

"It is what it is. I'm trying to help."

Walking back to the World of Coke, Jeremy thought about his petition. So far, when anyone back at camp had asked Stephen for legal advice, he'd snapped that he didn't work for free. Jeremy had a hunch that if he visited him at his office, it might go differently, but not today. He was numb from cold. The encroaching stupor put him in mind of the '93 blizzard, that historic storm when his mom had run out of orange juice—the only drink that let her swallow all her pills without gagging.

"Drink whiskey like a normal woman," his dad had said, and she set the pill bottles back down.

"What will happen now?" Jeremy had asked.

"My blood pressure will rise."

"Roads are impassable," his dad had said, which meant Jeremy could only trek alone through deep snow to Food City, where with stiff hands he selected a gallon of Tropicana. Carrying it uphill, he lost sensation in his fingers. He felt in service to something bigger. Back home, past dusk, he found his mother sitting in the dark. He flipped a switch, preparing for a swell of praise, but the power was out.

"Juice."

"That's sweet. No pulp?"

Jeremy looked down. *Lots of pulp*, the carton read. How had he forgotten that pulp made her gag like the pills did? It was suddenly all he remembered, along with his bank-breaking tonsillectomy, or the time he'd trampled her camellias. How had he been so mindless? She never asked, but he always wondered. Now, brushing snow off his car with a bare hand, he wondered too if he could trace all his bad luck back to that storm, when he'd thought he'd learned something. Perhaps everything he'd learned since then stood on a footing of that first wrong thing. His memory ceded no name for it, whatever it was. As he ran away, his mother had called out for him, too late; a blizzard yielded hiding places, and until they melted and were again exposed, he crouched in those holes like a gopher and never cried.

4.

In sixth grade, down below the gnat line where he was from, Patrick had sat quietly on the school bus every day for months while an eighth-grader pinched the Mexican boy's arms. She did it with glee, hard enough to leave welts. "This is for your own good," she would say, and "Look at you," until one day Patrick pushed her out the emergency door onto Moultrie Highway.

It wasn't about the Mexican boy; Patrick didn't care about that. It was that she reminded him of his uncle. To shove her helped take the sting out, and it got Patrick away from home. "Won't be too many Mexicans in there, but there's lots of blacks," his uncle had said on the way to reform school. Sure enough Patrick made friends with several, like his bunkmate Rooney, who played strategy games with him and ordered chess books through loan. For two years they learned every chess gambit, waiting for one of their own, namely the EF4 tornado that sucked up the perimeter wall and sent them fleeing in a car that Rooney hot-wired.

They drove it to Rooney's cousin's garage, where Patrick learned to detail cars with chamois leather and cotton swabs. He moved into Rooney's top bunk. Nights they rode around in Supras, Camaros, Firebirds, Chargers, Miatas, Talons, which took hours to clean—hours he already thought of as the best of his life. Better than reform school. There were about five billion people alive back then. As he cleaned, he imagined how it would be if not just he and Rooney but all five billion had Q-tips in hand, drying leather cream off their seats.

"It's almost like you enjoy washing cars," Rooney had said during one of their last games. "You look downright enraptured."

"Pays the bills," Patrick said, even as he decided to try to quit liking it. Rooney was his best friend, but he wasn't Rooney's; every month there were more and more folks to compete with.

"It's weird, and you don't have bills. You're fifteen."

"Saving for a rainy day."

"Wish you were saving for your own bedroom."

Some nights Rooney, Oliver, Zane, and Edgar couldn't squeeze him in to either front or back seats. "This is our special friend," they took to telling girls on nights when he did come. The girls, sizing him up, would giggle. Back at reform school, the only difference between him and Rooney had been their feelings about the place. Patrick had liked it, would have stayed. Only in solidarity had he gone along with Rooney's tornado gambit.

He made a deal with Rooney's cousin to move in above the garage. When he turned sixteen, he started driving the cars to Florida. One morning near Daytona he was pulled over for a faulty tail lamp. From detention he wrote Rooney five times and never heard back; still, Patrick imagined him rolling up on release day in a shiny car, with no one in back. "Ain't she sweet?" Rooney would say, and Patrick would nod blithely, but it was his own cousin who fetched him, in a Buick Century as filthy as the detention center.

He was eighteen by then. As his uncle's son guessed, he'd never been with a girl. There were places down the highway, his cousin told him—what kind did he want?

"Kind of place?"

"Kind of girl."

"What kinds are there?"

"You know, blonde? Fat?"

"Black," he said, and his cousin giggled like everyone had when Rooney called him a special friend.

At Headlights, slapping at gnats while bleach-blondes made love to their poles, Patrick imagined scouring the Century and then driving off to open a garage of his own, far from Tifton. "Pick." Something looked familiar about one who held the pole funny. Patrick pointed. She took him in back. They hadn't been talking for a minute before she started to yell.

What should he have done, Patrick complained to the police later; asked for ID? Blondes all looked alike. If he'd realized she was the bus girl, he might have only pinched her arm. A girl like her had a reason to shout on sight of him, but a stranger's shout proclaimed that the problem with him was general to all girls, and growing in size, so that last year any girl would have laughed but this year any girl would scream. And what about next year? What then? He found himself on top of her, covering her mouth. He screamed back. Choking her, he couldn't muffle her noise enough for the house music to drown it out. Even when the door opened, he didn't let go.

In adult prison he got shunted into the white gang, and it wasn't until he made parole that he learned that the offender camps were segregated too. When he arrived at an abandoned motor court off I-85, a black man he recognized from prison met him with a shotgun.

"I'll give you to the count of three."

"Look, I hung with those guys because I had to."

"Two and a half," the man said, chasing Patrick off to Acworth, where Gus gave him a tent because he looked like a nice guy.

On a pawn-shop Huffy he biked around applying at every auto detailing shop. Had he been convicted of a felony? Explain below. No one wanted him. Then Travis showed him the Jobs for

Felons list and he became a clerk at a Flying J. The car wash there was a drive-through with abrasive brushes that no one cleaned. Sometimes a girl would smile at him; he never knew why. He saved up to buy an '87 Fiero that never shone, no matter how he tried. Travis or Gus would invite him to play checkers, which left him feeling empty. One day, a week after the snow, two cops interrupted a game to say they would be shutting down the camp.

"You've got three days," they told Patrick, Allen, Gus, and Bruce, all sitting around the fire pit.

"You can't," Bruce said. "Why?"

"News gets out, you could be in danger."

"Where are we supposed to go?"

"I'll recommend a real estate agent."

After they left, Patrick's fingers still moved the checkers pieces, but in his mind his palms were joined in prayer. He asked for a signal, some glimpse of outcome. There was open country outside of Tifton where his uncle lived. Acres of emptiness, where no one could hear you. That wasn't the signal, though; that was his memory again.

He lay awake all night. The next day, two hours into his shift, Rooney walked up, wearing a UPS shirt that matched a truck at the pumps.

"Pack of Camel Lights," he said, eyes unfocused.

Rooney, it's Patrick, he thought of saying. You found me. I'm free.

Tobacco purchases required an ID check. If Patrick performed it, he could learn his old friend's address, go there later, even now. Rooney would ask where he stayed lately. Lake Allatoona? Got a boat dock? Boat? Bet you clean that boat with Q-tips—bet you enjoy it, and then the laughter, branding him a simpleton.

Bring it on, Patrick thought, it would be better than this.

Except he couldn't speak.

Reaching for Rooney's cigarettes, he considered how that girl on the bus must have felt, sitting beside him in the back room of that gentlemen's club without being known. What he'd done was try to stop her from screaming. It had felt like protecting himself, and now he saw she'd been protecting herself too.

He ran Rooney's card. Rooney signed. "Have a nice day," Patrick said, and went in back to fetch a bottle of Boone's.

He drank it down and opened another. "Anyone back there?" called a lady up front.

"Why, you horny?" he shouted back, quelling any need to return to the register.

Unplugging the security cameras, Patrick smiled at his joke. He was a sex offender who had never had sex: funny when you stopped to think. He stowed a case of Boone's in his pathetic old car. He ripped eye holes into one of his socks, pulled it over his head, drove around front, walked in, and announced that he had a gun.

Two of the customers sank to their knees. Patrick aimed a finger through his coat at the man still standing and said, "Key's in the drawer. Cash goes in a bag."

It was the easiest thing he'd ever done. "Wallets," he said, and they obeyed again. Folks did what you told them to. He drove home to Lake Allatoona, where he parked on the gravel below the bluff. The bag held eleven hundred dollars, more money than he'd possessed at once since working for Rooney's cousin. Back then he'd had a friend to spend it on. Find a new friend, he thought, except maybe that was when things had begun going wrong, when he'd bought Rooney a polo shirt and a CD.

Fuck it, he thought, wiping a splatter of mud from the car grille. He filled his backpack with bottles and hiked up to the fire pit.

"Who's that?" said a stiff corncob of a man, bucktoothed like Gus, sitting upright on a boulder. Patrick had never seen him.

"Your mom," he said, and fell into position beside Allen and Gus, who were roasting slabs of beef.

"Look who's shit-face drunk," Allen said.

"This is my cousin Garth," Gus said; "runs a quarry up in Rome."

"Four of your friends have done signed on," Garth told Patrick, "and I've got room for one more. No schools, no churches."

"His niggers quit all at once," Allen said, "like it was some kind of convention."

Patrick's pulse quickened. "You know what?" he said, feeling in his pockets, but he trailed off, wondering how the others knew he had quit too.

"See, it's like I was saying. Patrick don't fancy that word."

"We've all got our pet peeves," Garth said.

"I don't want some bitch on my work crew lawing me for how I talk."

"They aren't my friends," Patrick said.

"Do what?" Garth said.

"You said four of my friends have signed on. That's wrong."

"Look, bub. Day after tomorrow, cops will ask your intended residence. If you ain't got one, they'll take you into custody."

It must be only a coincidence, Patrick thought. While he'd been robbing the store, they'd been drinking here by this fire.

"How do you know what words I like?"

"You paid a visit to the Sweetwater Creek Motor Court," Allen said, as Stephen ambled over and sat down.

"I go where I please," said Patrick, certain Allen could only have learned about that from the cops.

The cops must have gone to shut the other camp down too, and then laughed with the white campers about it.

"Well, why'd they leave?" Patrick asked.

"He means your niggers," Allen said. Garth grinned; Gus bit his lip. They would rather be allied with the cops than with the other camp.

Earlier Patrick had thought Rooney's visit to the Flying J was his sign, but Rooney had been only a prelude. Patrick walked to Stephen's tent. The .45-caliber revolver from Stephen's briefcase fit snugly in his coat pocket. As he returned to the fire, he heard Allen saying, "This one's a bookworm. Too smart for your quarry."

"Maybe Garth's old employees were too smart for his quarry," Patrick said.

"Maybe you're shit-face drunk," Allen said.

"Maybe I don't want somebody solving your problems."

"You mean you don't want somebody solving yours?" Allen replied, reaching for the sizzling steak with a bare hand.

Allen had always given Patrick the creeps. His drawl, his leer, his dirty old Cavalier. The way his grimy fingers clutched meat while he gnawed at it like a squirrel. "Try this," he said, offering the steak as if there was no conflict, and Patrick thought, Be with the guys who will have you. Go where you're wanted. He played the idea out a few moves ahead. A quarry would be a filthy place to work. He didn't like these guys. The only good work he'd done was on cars, cleaning them inch by inch with his friends.

"No, solving yours," he said, and shot Garth in the temple.

Garth gasped, fell forward. Almost immediately Patrick could smell the flames singeing him. You couldn't make people want you. Aside from that, though, you could do as you pleased. His uncle had taught him that much. What he pleased to do now was give the others a mess to clean up. Earlier he'd intended to go into the woods first. But watching Allen and Gus drag Garth away, he pictured them dragging him too. Explaining to the cops why he was covered in their fingerprints. Three black cops hearing Allen stumble through a tale of their bloody teamwork: that was too tempting an endgame to pass up. He picked up Allen's steak from where he'd dropped it, had a bite, licked his lips clean, aimed, fired, lost his balance, shut his eyes, and never hit the ground.

5.

For three days, while the other campers disregarded the warning he delivered from the cop downtown, Jeremy left voicemails for Georgia Interstate Compact saying he'd planned to wait and move in the new year but now the timeline was out of his hands. "The police are worried about my safety," he said, "so I'm hoping you guys are worried too." He expected no answer, nor was he surprised that no one at camp believed him. It had to do with the shape of his face, the strange sheen of his eyes: people just didn't trust him. Teachers, cops, the fathers of girls. Once he'd overheard an English tourist at work tell her friend he looked wanton. In Alaska, he thought, his ushanka and balaclava would help hide that.

On the third day he came home from the World of Coke to find the guys discussing where to go. Cumberland Island and live off shrimping. The Oconee Forest and hunt for deer. You did right by us, he waited for someone to tell him. Sorry for not trusting you.

"Still going to Alaska, wild boy?"

"Waiting to hear back."

"Let's all go," Bruce said. "Gus can drive us in his bus."

"I got laid by a pretty fine Alaska girl," said Allen.

"Just don't tell Stephen. He'll light our bus up with a Molotov cocktail."

For another whole day Jeremy stared at his phone, until it occurred to him that neither response—approved, denied—would answer the question he had been hanging on.

Forty-five minutes later he was on the eastern perimeter, parking at a nearly abandoned strip mall where he found Brick, Butter, and Younce nestled between a gospel church and a military recruiting center.

"Hello?" he called, standing before an unmanned desk in a low room lined with faux-wood paneling. The place looked like a den of shysters.

"Jeremy?" asked Stephen when he emerged, sounding unsure of his name.

"I'm wondering what happens if I violate a restraining order."

"Depends on who took the order out."

"Father of the fifteen-year-old I slept with," Jeremy said. He knew how Stephen felt about the men at camp, and he wasn't going to downplay his crime.

"If you write her a letter, I could deliver it."

Stephen was staring hungrily at Jeremy, who'd seen that look before—from across the circle, from across the fire. He could smell alcohol. For only one reason did anyone help anyone, and it had as little to do with Jeremy himself as the AA groups' hatred did.

"Just tell me how long I'd go to jail."

"You're on parole, right?"

He nodded, suddenly ashamed of bringing such an obvious question in. "I only asked because I was passing by on the way to a meeting."

"You pass five feet from my tent every day," said Stephen. He probably thought Jeremy was lying, which for once Jeremy was doing.

"That reminds me, the cops came to confirm what I told everybody Monday."

"Yeah, and you attacked a kid in Savannah wearing Mickey Mouse ears."

"Okay, well," Jeremy said.

"Who will you be this afternoon?"

"Not you; you're different," he said, another lie. He had read about Stephen at work. It was a good story. He could act it out.

Stephen was nodding. "There are tiers," he said. "There's us, and there's everyone else."

"I feel the same," Jeremy said, standing to go.

"I'll find out by tomorrow about your restraining order."

Jeremy thanked him and left. He navigated the access road with care, breathing as deliberately as he could. Not until he'd merged onto the highway did he floor it, stereo on fifty, screaming along to a Björk song's dissonant chords. She could distort his world into icy echoes that sealed him inside a blue crevasse, but not today. He aimed his hood ornament at the skyline and soon he was in Little Five Points, parking at the Fishers', where Melissa answered in a leather jacket, holding a Siamese cat.

Her auburn hair was so stylishly coiffed that Jeremy gasped. "You're ringing my bell," she said, as the cat scrambled to escape.

"I've loved you all this time. You're all I've got. Don't shout." How often had he rehearsed the lines that fell out of him like lead pellets? Speaking them, he got the sensation that he knew the wrong meaning of love, that that was the wrong thing he'd learned back in the blizzard.

"Your camp's in the news," Melissa replied.

She might as well have slapped his face. He wanted to slap her back. His mind wasn't in his head; it was in his arm, slapping her. Just in time, he grabbed that arm with his other hand, and nodded toward a diploma on the mantel.

"Congratulations," he said.

"Yeah, I'd have graduated no matter what."

No matter how many times you hurt me, Jeremy thought, but he said, "I've come to apologize," telling his third lie of the day, the one most likely to draw Melissa out of her father's house.

He gestured up the block, where too many people were gardening for her to claim any threat. "Two minutes," she said, slipping on her shoes.

The first half-minute he squandered on silence while waiting to escape any possible earshot or sight line. When they got to the main shopping street, he said, "I'm moving."

"Me too, for a master's in social work."

To help abuse victims like yourself, he thought, hating Melissa again for being so smug. For not asking where he was moving. For pretending she'd never loved him. Spending the summer in Seville, after the trouble she'd caused by applying there. Finding a Spanish boyfriend, learning a language from him and God knew what else. He swallowed the anger, took her by the shoulders and said, "I'll never stop loving you."

They had stopped beside a newsstand. "Here's what I was talking about," Melissa said, so flippantly that she could have punctuated herself by blowing a bubble.

A headline read, "Homeless Sex Offenders Pitch Camp in Wild," above a picture of Allen's tent.

"Dad's still kind of obsessed. He followed you there, then he went to the cops and they're closing it."

"I see," Jeremy said. He walked on. After seven years, he was still a puppet on her dad's string, and so was she and that was that.

The only way to force her into an emotion was to have a panic attack.

It wasn't a decision so much as it was simply destined to happen. Kneeling on the sidewalk amid dog-walking couples, he held steady against the air. "Breathe," Melissa said, jostling him. He shivered at that touch, the first in seven years, but took in no air. She shook harder. "Inhale!" she cried, full of concern.

His plan was working. All he had to do now was stop loving her.

It ought to be easy, with this new face to match to his old memories. He'd always fancied underdogs. His mom and dad; the Braves until they bought their way to first; Melissa, stammering through her testimony that day at Alateen when they had met. Crying about her dad the goner and all he'd squandered. She wasn't an underdog anymore. He took the face begging him to breathe and put it to the time at Burger King when he'd had only three dollars, the evening after they'd buried his own father. What if we share a Whopper and a Coke, he'd asked, but she'd wanted her own Whopper and her own Coke. "You're the dumbass who forgot the money," she had said.

As he imagined her chewing that hamburger, the light ebbed. Selfishness was innate, it didn't come from being young.

He awoke beside a juniper bush with Melissa squeezing his hand, crying. He stood up. "Go home," he said. "You're too old for me now."

"Not falling for that," she said, in pursuit not toward her house but Patrick's car, which he'd already pointed toward I-75, which stretched north to Canada, where he could bear west across the boreal forest for five thousand miles.

If he reached that forest, he thought, walking faster, his luck had turned.

"I know how you try to make people hate you."

"It's been two minutes."

"Where will you go when they close it?"

"Told you. Alaska."

"You only said *moving*. Ask where I'm moving."

"I'm not attracted to women your age."

"Do you even have a job lined up?"

"No, ask your dad to lend me some money," he said—a funny joke, given that Mr. Fisher really had spent tens of thousands of dollars to try and send Jeremy away forever. The best things were free, he thought, smiling in farewell. Her lip was quivering when he turned away, so he never knew if she acknowledged the irony before turning toward home.

6.

The name on Allen's birth certificate was Al Jack Downey, Jr., after his dad, who'd been named for two minor-league all-stars. At school Allen liked bragging on Jack's 100-mph shine ball and Al's 600-foot home runs. He said he'd met Michael Jackson and his mom was Robert E. Lee's great-grandniece. It got to where other kids called bullshit even on the truth. "If those dudes and your grandpa was so good, why didn't they reach the majors?" By then Allen's grandpa was dead along with his other grandparents. His mom was in New Mexico; his dad was locked up. No one around could confirm or deny anything, and Allen resolved to go look for Jack and Al himself someday.

The year he learned to drive, he found Al, the shortstop, in a pine shack in the Okefenokee Wilderness. Huge, blind, and one-footed, Al believed it was 1989. "Living in the future, old man," said Allen, to which Al croaked, "You're living in the past."

"Why didn't you reach the majors?"

"Who wants to know?"

"Were you blackballed?"

"Are you the police?"

"I'm Davy Downey's grandson."

"I couldn't hit for shit, but I was better than him."

"Baseball was only his hobby," Allen said, compelled to lie even to bedraggled strangers. "He gave it up once he won the welterweight championship."

Six hours north, on a high heath bald near Rabun Gap, Allen knocked on the door of a square pine shack like Al's, as if they'd helicoptered Al's up while he was en route. Jack was supposed to be eighty, but the kid who answered was no more than twenty, rail-thin, bottle in hand, joint in his mouth.

"Who are you?" he said, and Allen said he'd come to shake hands with the pitcher he was named for.

"That's me," the skinny kid said, and Allen thought, You're living in the past. Then the kid said, "Joke, he's dead."

"Since when?"

"Other day."

"Is that gin?"

"Have a taste."

The boy invited Allen into a room whose four windows faced down four slopes. Woods, woods, woods, town, and in the town window sat a girl whose green eyes Allen stared into until she was offering to give him head.

Her name was Eulalia, the boy's cousin and Jack's grandchild. Let them call bullshit on this, Allen thought, leaning against the pine wall. "I'm his grandkid too, in a way," he said, stoned by then. They tripped together, hit after hit, day after day, until Jack's acid was almost gone. He said he bought it by the sheet in

Nashville once a month and sold hits for five bucks. "I could sell a sheet a week," Allen said, knowing he couldn't. Jack phoned in an order quintuple the usual size. In a grand finale they ate five hits apiece and hit the road. Allen drove. Whole cyclones of rain poured down, and mastodons roamed the highway, but what wrecked them and killed Jack was a broken axle.

"I'm a world-class driver," he stood there telling Eulalia in the cold rain; "NASCAR's recruiting me."

For a little while, she quit blaming him. Holding hands on the shore of Lake Ocoee, they vowed never to part, but then she was asking if he would ever have an abortion. It was apropos of nothing. "I'm a dude," he said, as rain flowed down the bank, or was she crying? She seemed to be sliding away with the water.

"Our mom wanted to get rid of us."

"You were twins?" he asked, astonished.

"No, we were four years apart."

As the sirens approached, Allen saw into her question and understood what she meant: because of his mind, combined with his driving, his search for some failed namesake, his mom should have gotten rid of him.

"I don't even know your last name," he called to Eulalia as they dragged him away, hoping his tears would make it to the river.

Every day of five years, Allen would look up to where Brushy Mountain loomed over the prison of that name. On it stood a stone cottage where a ravishing gypsy observed the prison yard through a silver spyglass. "She likes guys like you," said Allen's cellmate, who'd been with her on furlough.

"I've dropped in on the stone lady, too," Allen replied. No matter what you claimed in prison, it was real. He said he'd had twenty-eight girls from twenty-five states. His fellows were so pleased in that brag that he decided to render it true.

"Where's she from?" he asked one day in the yard, gesturing to the mountain. His cellmate gestured the same.

"But what state was she born in?"

"Is that the first thing you ask all your girls?"

"Sure," Allen said, heart racing. How you got to be the best, you said something and then you did it. Every day the sun reflected off the stone lady's window and he waved. In March 1993, when they set him free, he walked the main road to a gravel drive up the mountain. When he reached the summit clearing, the sun was sinking over the plateau. Ready to knock, he stopped in his tracks: the cottage wasn't a house, only some sheets of propped-up plywood painted to look like stones.

He kicked them onto a pile of gaffing lights soaking in mud. It was almost dark. Counting blow jobs, he'd been with girls from only two states. He was done with that number, and rode an old bicycle downhill into Wartburg to take his first girl.

"You should feel glad to have a man like me," he told Cheryl, who'd lived her whole life in Tennessee.

She drove him to Harriman, where every woman he talked to came from there. He hitched down 27 past Chattanooga and across the line, where he met Infinity. If Infinity had lived in Tennessee, he might have returned to a prison whose inmates knew him for a fool, but the inmates at Hays State didn't know a thing. That was where he met Travis. "I've been with girls from thirty-six states," he told Travis, who replied, "My goal's to get with every pretty girl in one state."

Upon parole they shared an apartment. He got a job selling cars. In 2006 a school opened across the road, and then the law passed in 2007. They made their way to an outdoor outfitters to shoplift some tents. Allen's, a Marmot, may have saved his life. If he'd bought one instead of stealing it, he wouldn't have been able to afford flame-retardant cloth—not that he'd been looking for that feature; he only chose the warmest one. He knew winters would be no joke. The night of the fire, the temperature dropped to eleven while they argued about what to do with the bodies of Garth and Patrick. Travis said it would need to be twenty below to keep them from putrefying. Gus countered that if eviction was coming tomorrow anyway, so what?

For once Allen didn't take Travis's side. Who cared? He'd stopped seeing the point of Georgia. As long as he lived in camp, his number would remain two. Georgia and Tennessee. Down at the car lot lately the guys were calling bullshit. He imagined the campers did too, at least in their heads. Looked up team rosters from the years he gave. "Screw it, they can smell or not smell," he told Bruce, and went in his tent to think back on the stone lady. If she'd been up there where she was supposed to be, he might never have touched anyone else. Was she on Eulalia's mountain, laughing at him out four windows through a silver spyglass? Fuck that bitch, he was thinking as he came. Then he unstaked his tent. Waiting for everyone else to fall asleep, he passed out too. He awoke to flames, closer than the campfire.

Two of the tents were burning.

Without a moment's thought, Allen rolled down the bluff, tent and all, past strange voices. He landed inches from the lakeshore. He untangled himself and saw pickup trucks and a police cruiser parked near his car. They were empty; no one saw him drive away for good. Blasting the heat, hugging curves like a stockcar driver, he thought of a new story, *I saved six men from a fire,* but as it turned out, besides Jeremy—who'd vanished—he was the only one who hadn't survived to hear the news.

"The men at those camps got a preview of hellfire," said a state representative on the TV above Allen's barstool at Waffle House.

There had been injuries, and some loud guys to the left were chuckling about it. "I had a cousin burn to death in Iraq," the waitress told them. "Not what I'd call funny."

"You feel sorry for them?" one of the guys asked.

"One used to come in for omelets. This lawyer. He was sweet to me."

"Probably hoped you had a daughter."

She shrugged as if maybe the man was right, which of course he was. Stop being so naïve, Allen wanted to tell her. Only fools trust sweet. You'll get yourself hurt.

He chewed his toast, and the news moved on to the continuing saga of Michael Vick, en route to US District Court for sentencing.

"These Falcons, their time is up," said one of the men.

"Their time was up years ago," the waitress said. She drifted over and refilled Allen's coffee. "You look wistful, mister. Penny for your thoughts."

"Just eager to get back on the road."

"Where you headed, all by yourself?"

"All over the place," he said, wondering if they were flirting like normal people. He wasn't sure; still, even in the wake of the fire, the chance felt good. "I've only ever been to two of the fifty states. Figure it's time to see the country."

7.

Alone in his office after Jeremy left, Stephen pulled up records of Jeremy's 2001 statutory rape case on LexisNexis for the second time. He read more closely than before. Mid-trial the kid had fired his expensive lawyer and pled nolo contendere. Stephen didn't get it. Why didn't Jeremy want people to like him? If a protective order was still in place from back then, it was permanent. To break it would commit a new crime, which Jeremy surely knew, which meant he was lying to Stephen, scoping out details for Act Two in the strange performance piece playing out in the addiction recovery rooms of Greater Atlanta.

Cancel the show by phoning ahead to the Fisher household, thought Stephen—but he was no rat. He only wanted to teach the boy a lesson.

He screen-captured eighteen-year-old Jeremy's mug shot and saved it with his other pictures, then drove downtown to defend a woman accused of stealing a purse. She didn't show. The court ruled against her, in favor of a department store that had spent more money prosecuting her than the purse had cost. Who cared? Not Stephen. Nothing was at stake; she was just another broke woman. He went to Vickery's for martinis, one two three four. In the parking lot afterward, the flags of America and Georgia rippled in the wind. On a truck bumper a third flag announced *Power of Pride*, although pride was a sin. Cover it with one that said *Sin of Pride*, he thought, driving away.

On the radio some woman was interviewing a theologian. "Do you consider Muhammad to have been a pacifist like Jesus?"

"I do not consider Jesus to have been a pacifist," the theologian answered. "Jesus drove out the money changers with a cord whip and said, *What I offer is the sword.*"

Before getting on the highway Stephen bought a six-pack of Heineken. He drank one on I-75 and then another on Glade Road before he arrived home. *Home.* He needed a new word for the place. Then again, Jeremy had said the evictions were real.

He ought to be happy about it, but as he climbed the hill, he didn't want to believe it.

Ignoring the eternal campfire, where the guys sat talking to a stranger, Stephen fetched a towel from the line. He undressed under the oak and righted the upended jug with the holes in it. After tying the dangling rope to the bottleneck he pulled it until the jug hung above him. He looped it around a branch. Water was spilling out, muddying the dirt. He opened another beer. It was about fifty out, maybe the last day before spring when a shower would feel bearable. Humming a tune, he scrubbed himself. A bird chirped. As it flew away, Stephen turned to see Bruce running off with his clothes and his towel.

Dripping dry, he devised a hateful lie to tell the D.A. about Bruce. About everyone. Then he stalked naked to his tent and found the clothes baskets gone too.

Behind him he heard giggling, and backed out to find Allen, Travis, Gus, Bruce, and the bucktoothed stranger all gathered there. He cupped his hands over his cock, and they laughed harder.

"It don't bother us," Bruce said. "Be naked. Don't you like to?"

"Or we're too old to be naked in front of," Gus said, causing more eruptions.

Letting his hands fall, Stephen stood there as casually as he could. He wanted his demeanor to convey that he still had friends in high places, and that those high-placed friends would come fuck everybody up.

"Dude, your clothes is under the sycamore," Bruce said. "We were just having fun."

Bending to pick up a tree branch, Stephen focused in on Bruce's pouty eyes.

"I mean, how about a laugh?"

"Keep the clothes. You're right, I like being naked."

"So you opened those curtains on purpose."

"The bus came each day at seven and three," Stephen said, and right away the offenders' trance was as rapt as any angry jury's.

He had them. "There was a girl named Piper with coppery hair and a blue backpack," he said, thinking maybe he understood what Jeremy had been doing at meetings. He'd been proving people's sheer gall to believe.

"And?"

"And this," he said, swinging the tree branch like a bat toward Bruce's head. But it was so rotten that it broke in midair.

"I'm not one of you," he said, while Bruce laughed. "What I just said was a lie."

"It's the truth according to Georgia."

"I'm leaving Georgia."

"If you don't know reciprocity, you're a shitty lawyer."

"That's only with bordering states," he said, a bigger lie than the high-placed friends or the bus. He'd had the friends; the bus had come at the hours he'd named, even if there was no Piper, no girl, no boy, no one but Seamus.

They left him alone to pull on his pajamas, but he was too drunk to be alone. He carried a beer to the fire, where the others were talking about some quarry.

So Jeremy had been telling the truth.

He sat down opposite Gus, who turned and said, "Look, dude," cutting his bucktoothed twin off midsentence. "Most days you won't even talk to us."

"I was framed by a judge. You're rapists."

"How do you know I wasn't framed?"

"Were you framed?"

"Why should I tell you?"

Stephen tried to think of a clever answer. None came. He thought of replying that there was a bathhouse called the Downtown Men's Club, where after Seamus died he took to sitting in the pitch-black darkroom. With nothing left to live for, you were free to go where you wanted and pursue hard dreams. Seamus had jumped without even trying—unless his hard dream had been sobriety—but Stephen was ready to try. Even after posting bail, he kept it up. After a month he knew the regulars by the feel of their bodies. Sometimes in the locker room he saw faces, too, like the corporate lawyer's who'd beaten him in a suit over swing sets. Baxter Philpotts. About once a week Baxter sucked Stephen off in the darkroom and didn't know. One day Baxter showed up with the judge assigned to Stephen's case, a round redhead named Harold Hawkins. They were soaking in the hot tub when they saw Stephen passing by. The judge pursed his lips, and Stephen smiled. The slightest smile back might have meant *join us*, but neither man gave up that gesture, and Stephen was left to wonder upon conviction if the encounter was his true crime.

"Are you gonna answer?"

"I forget the question, but I imagine the answer is I don't care," he was saying when he heard footsteps. Good, he thought, having chosen what to tell Jeremy. Forget Alaska. You're on the no-fly list and if you drive they won't issue a passport. Then he would sit back and watch Jeremy grapple with never going north. It would serve as punishment not only for portraying Stephen in the meetings but for being young, for having a future.

This, said a voice in Stephen's head, was how he treated the people he liked.

The footsteps weren't Jeremy's after all, but Patrick's.

During the pandemonium, Stephen guzzled one of Patrick's malt beverages. I don't care, he kept telling himself every second of the next hour. If he hadn't been drunk or in shock, he might have fled. For safety, for good. Mourning the deaths of child molesters didn't involve him. Dragging their bodies around. Planning what to do. Bruce proposed pitching camp deeper in the woods. Allen said he could find a fair-minded official to hear their case. "Practice Gandhian nonviolence," Stephen suggested, just to make fun, as they burbled on.

Had they not heard him? Should he take further offense?

To prove once and for all that he wasn't a part of them, he brought out a book, hastily chosen from his stacks. *The Confusions of Young Törless*. Too drunk to read, he opened it randomly and moved his eyes over the words. *There had always been something that his thoughts could not get the better of, something that seemed at once so simple and so strange. There had been pictures in his mind that were not really pictures at all.*

Before he could learn whose thoughts, or pictures of what, Bruce snatched the book away and tossed it into the fire.

Stephen turned from Bruce's soft, pudgy face, which appeared amused even in anger, toward the flames engulfing *Young Törless*. The spine curled and was gone.

"Somebody's got to show you how it is," Bruce said.

Intending to throw a punch, Stephen stood up. Bruce's face was shaped that way from having no shame. Without shame, you could grin and crack jokes. You could hide people's clothes, wonder where sports stars would live. Bruce had probably been born that way, plus it didn't hurt to ignore the past. The sickly mother he'd been avenging in Savannah had recently died. Never again would Bruce weaken to think of her, whereas Stephen's mother was alive and well in Augusta, in the house he'd grown up in. She had thrown legendary Masters parties there until Stephen's arrest. "When you were gay," she'd said, "I didn't mind, but this?"

He'd called his mother callow, but those socialites had been her friends. It hurt when friends took themselves away from you. You wanted to hurt them back, or you were liable to hurt yourself instead. After Seamus died, when he knew he'd be feeling no more pleasure anyway, he purchased enough cocaine to use up his serotonin for good, and snorted it for a week. When it was gone, he poured a whole coffee bag into one filter and tapped *brew*, hoping to make his heart burst. Waiting, he grew ripe with sweat. Wasn't it December? He undressed and opened every window. Raising the last one to the icy wind, he heard a pop. Steam was rising from the griddle. He'd forgotten to fill the reservoir.

He went to unplug the machine, remove the pot. As one noise dwindled, another grew: a bus—he could see it out the living room window, pulling up.

Where he stood, he was invisible, but the situation was too interesting not to respond to. Heart racing as he'd wished, he crossed to the front of the house, until the bus wasn't thirty feet away. *Atlanta Public Schools.* High schoolers, middle schoolers; either way the boys in back were the ones to watch. The very day he died, Seamus talked about boozing in the back of the bus, getting high for the first time, in severe contrast to Stephen's stifled childhood when he'd wanted daily to give up his forlorn front seat. The boys in back had sensed his yearning, turned against him, those same kids staring now. Carafe in hand, he stared back. Look at me, fuckers; I'm a trial lawyer. He was too old to envy them, he knew. He knew to envy Seamus was to misread Seamus's story. A girl approached the bus stairs from inside. It was her stop. Had he been ogling her all year? Your Honor, he never even learned his neighbors' names. The driver warned her back in. They went chugging on down the road. Blind strings in one hand, pot handle dangling from the other, Stephen wondered what he'd meant to do.

He stood by the fire, wondering. "Show me," he said, replying to what Bruce seemed to have already forgotten saying.

THE NINETY-FIFTH PERCENTILE

THE DAY THE HONDURAN BOY showed back up in American History instead of vanishing with his deported parents, Caidin Maddox convinced his friends Jeff and Adam to follow him home from school. The boy, Juaco Luna, had been wearing the same three T-shirts all spring. His shoes had holes, he carried no backpack. That wasn't why Caidin stared at Juaco's smooth brown arms and slender frame all through class, but it gave him an excuse to be curious. Everyone else at their West Houston magnet school, though it was technically open to teens of any income bracket who tested above the ninety-fifth IQ percentile, owned a few weeks' rotation of shirts.

Waiting for Juaco in Adam's Z4, the boys discussed the driver's exam. Caidin would be sixteen in June, and Jeff wasn't far behind.

"Don't study," Adam said. "That test is designed for the other ninety-four percent. Jeff, when do you get your Viper?"

"Starting to think Corvette, so me and Caidin can have matching ones."

"Awesome," Caidin lied. He hadn't told his friends the sad terms of his deal: the Corvette would come the day he joined the Air Force—same as his brother Caleb, who'd earned a Porsche by signing up.

Jeff glanced at Juaco's decade-old Chrysler LeBaron. "I'd take cabs to school before I'd drive that thing."

"Mexicans like old cars," Adam said. "They won't ride in a new car."

"He's Honduran, but remind me why we care?"

As Caidin sought an excuse for why, Milo Hux, the pale waif who'd founded the gay-straight alliance, walked with Juaco to the LeBaron and opened the passenger door.

"Now do you get it?" he said.

His friends did. They tailed the LeBaron to a Sugar Land mansion near Adam's, where the car disappeared behind a gate. "You've got to admit this is some shit," Caidin said, and they agreed, but back at Jeff's it was like they'd already forgotten. "Bet they're sucking each other" drew only a chuckle. When Caidin said, "I bet the gay suicide hotline's on his speed-dial," they were too focused on Xbox to laugh at all.

By the time of the yearbook staff meeting the next day, Caidin was bursting to talk about Juaco somehow. He didn't want to speak ill of anyone, per se, but he couldn't go singing Juaco's praises. All he could think to do was announce, "Milo Hux and Juaco Luna share a bed and Milo's hiding him from ICE," which seemed to do the job.

A week later, Juaco quit coming to class. The week after that, Caidin's mother looked up from the PTA newsletter and said, "Do you know the boy who got deported?" Caidin shook his head. When she passed him the pamphlet, his eyes fell to where an

Agent Bret Garrity of US Immigration and Customs Enforcement, same last name as the yearbook copy editor, said he respected the PTA's opinion about Juaco Luna Ochoa but the law was the law.

The removal would have happened anyway, Caidin was telling himself when he spotted Milo at lunch, eating alone. The law was the law. Every time he came close to Milo, he repeated that to himself, feeling gradually better, until the day his brother phoned from Lackland to ask their mom to drive the Porsche while he was overseas.

"It's too small for my trips to Austin," said Mrs. Maddox, a state senator. "Caidin, maybe you could take over. But the first sign you're being foolish, we'll garage it." ·

It was like he'd been pumped full of speed. Unable to believe his luck, he hugged his mom, shook his dad's hand. The last day of school, as his brother was landing in Anbar Province, he scored ninety-eight on the driving test. To celebrate, he drove his friends all over town. The faster he went, the more adrenaline he had. Soon Jeff got his Corvette. Every day they prowled in someone's car. They cruised at the Galveston Seawall. One day Adam phoned to say he was bringing Milo Hux along to SplashTown, "since he's just up the road."

"Homo say what?" Caidin said, uneasy.

"Just for someone to make fun of, you know."

On the way to the water park Milo kept making eyes with Caidin as if he knew the truth. Caidin adjusted the mirror so Milo couldn't see, but then he couldn't see Milo either and he put it back. At one point Milo announced that he'd lied to his parents about where he was; they believed he was taking the SAT. "It's weird someone like you has parents," Caidin said.

Jeff and Adam giggled. Encouraged by their laughter, Caidin picked at Milo all day—holding his head below water more than once, tossing his ice cream into the lazy river, even telling some jocks that Milo had a crush on them.

Over and over his friends cracked up. It seemed like even Milo was stifling laughter, until he said, "You treat me like a dog."

"Hey, we were just having fun," Jeff said.

"Yeah, think of it like an initiation," Adam said.

"Except I'm nicer than this to dogs," said Caidin, afraid his friends were wussing out. When everyone around you was gifted, it was hard to excel. Even in Caidin's percentile he intended to be best at two things: driving fast and making fun of gay boys. "I won't brake till you cry *uncle*," he said on the drive home, weaving through traffic at ninety miles an hour. On the shoulder he zoomed past a slow bus. Veering back into his lane, a glance in the rearview presented Milo, tranquil as a monk, gazing serenely west.

Caidin observed Milo's strange sublimity, waiting for eye contact again, until Jeff shouted his name. They were hurtling toward a semi.

He stomped on the brake, skidded, regained control. "Why didn't you cry *uncle*?" he said as they all caught their breath.

"I suppose I wasn't paying attention," Milo said dreamily, as if he didn't quite know where he was.

In July Caidin's mother looked up from another newsletter and asked, "Do you know a Milo Hux?" It seemed that a Milo Hux had flipped his car on the Gulf Freeway and died.

"He was doing ninety-five. Tell me you know it's idiocy, going that fast."

"Mom, on the Autobahn in Germany—"

"It's idiocy there, too! You'd throw your life away for a fast car ride?"

"I promise I won't die," Caidin said, which upset her more

until he revised his words to say, "I promise I won't drive like what's-his-name."

Without asking Jeff and Adam along, he sped toward the coast. He knew his friends would blame him for Milo. No one understands me, he thought, almost happy in the idea, touching himself while he drove. He bet Caleb was jerking off in his Strike Eagle. Almost to Surfside Beach, his phone rang. It was Jeff. "Hey, faggot," he answered, relieved.

"I bought *Poisoned Wasteland*. Can you be here in half an hour?"

Jeff's house was sixty miles away. In places the speed limit would dip as low as thirty, and there were traffic lights. "Don't see why not."

"Bring those games I lent you."

"I'll try," he said, jerking the wheel hard left across the center line. He set a new course. Feeling sorry for people who'd died before there were cars, he floored it. He hoped his body would never run out of adrenaline.

"Took you long enough," Jeff said forty-eight minutes later.

"Yeah, I was south of Freeport when you called."

"Caidin, shut up."

"Porsches are faster than Chevrolets," he said with a shrug, sitting down to play Jeff's new game. Their characters, deformed mutants who'd survived a nuclear war, wandered a dead zone in search of elixir. The fastest they could walk was four miles an hour. To circumnavigate the game world would take a thousand game hours, ten real hours. Caidin didn't see why his dumb, trudging avatar couldn't at least ride a bike.

"Let's go driving," he said, over the game's screaming metalcore theme music.

"You know, cars are okay, but they're not my life."

"You know, you used to be fun to hang out with."

"Doesn't Milo get you to thinking?"

Caidin's blood went leaden. "What is your life, then? Video games?"

"My life's bigger than one thing, Caidin."

"Why would speedometers go to 120 if we shouldn't drive 120?"

Jeff didn't seem to have an answer. Whatever, thought Caidin, pushing himself upright. His mutant stood still. He swung his foot. The death growls and guitar riffs ceased. *NO INPUT*, said a blue screen after the Xbox had hit the wall, and then he was flying west on the Katy Freeway.

He bought an eighth of weed from his brother's dealer. To cruise around smoking it felt way better than sitting in Jeff's bedroom. Tousling his bangs, he looked in the rearview. He would grow his hair out, install new subwoofers, and buy a whole ounce when the eighth was gone. He did all three. High on the first day of school, he sat in back with crossed arms like some regular middle-quartile kid. When teachers called his name, he waited a few seconds before saying "Here." People liked it. There was a blonde girl named Astrid who reminded him of a seahorse. Every day he would catch her glancing at him. After a week he was holding her hand. She was friends with some jocks who'd turned to drugs. At the Galleria after school they all ate sugar-cube acid together. Hank, the second-string quarterback, climbed the Water Wall with his girlfriend Izzy, laughing as the police pulled them down. That was the trick—not to care. They piled into the Porsche, whose wheel felt alive: Caidin had only to think of steering, and the car sped onto I-610.

"Beach?" he asked, thinking he'd get them there faster than ever. Here was his chance to show how little he cared.

"It's too hot for shirts," said Izzy, pulling hers off. "Astrid, hold the wheel."

When Caidin took his shirt off too, they cheered as if he'd shed his training wheels. Half-naked they played Twenty Questions, Izzy going first. An animal, in Texas, bigger than the car, and there was only one.

"Your mom," he said. Izzy laughed. On his new friends' wavelength, he could set the cruise control at seventy and restrain the urge to prove what he was made of.

"Shamu," said Hank, and Izzy said yes. They kissed.

"Every SeaWorld has a Shamu," Caidin said. "When one dies, they capture another one and name it Shamu."

"There's other SeaWorlds?" said Astrid, who had stopped looking like a seahorse to him. It didn't matter. He stole glimpses of Hank in the mirror, stole more of them at the beach, sitting on sand in their underwear as derricks swayed.

"There's a hurricane out there," Izzy said, which Caidin took to be a metaphor.

"Did you know Juaco Luna?" he asked her.

"Yeah, he kissed me, and it was amazing. Hank, if Juaco Luna comes back from El Salvador, I'm dumping you."

"He's from Honduras," Caidin said, wishing he hadn't asked. They stared out to sea, Astrid's hand feeling like warm dough in his. "Storm's coming," Izzy said again. Say what you mean, Caidin thought, but it turned out to be real. Back at Hank's they watched it assault the Gulf Coast. New Orleans was five hours east, three if you drove like Caidin, and he suggested going to see it. Instead they smoked pot and lay on Astrid's bed. When she touched him, pretending to like it was easy; he just touched her back in the same places. After two days of that, he asked when they would be returning to school.

"School's out of the question."

"We're in the ninety-fifth percentile," he said.

Hank and the girls looked at each other and giggled.

"My parents got me in," Hank said, "just like yours got you in."

"No, I'm in the ninety-eight-point-fourth percentile," said Caidin, feeling a sudden urge to see his mother.

He made up an excuse to leave. But when he arrived home, he found a note for him and the maid that the Maddoxes were in Dallas.

Smoking a joint, he searched Diaryland for boys named Juaco—nothing—and then Milo—dozens, all alive. He searched for ones who wanted to kill themselves, and these were easy to find. Every other boy on Diaryland wished to die. Their heroes were Kurt Cobain, Jim Morrison, the kid who'd perished on a bus in Alaska. Most wrote with indistinguishable dreamy fatalism, but one called Timescale aspired to a wholly original death: floating in a balloon into a wildfire; sailing to Antarctica to walk nude into its tundra; coating himself with sugar and lying down among fire ants. Caidin tried to concoct some outlandish methods of his own to post in a comment. He couldn't come up with any, and besides, Timescale would ask why he wanted to die, when he wanted only to talk. He dialed his brother's number. Busy bombing Ramadi, Caleb didn't answer, not like Caleb was any fun anyway. If he were home, he would only be drinking vodka with his stupid girlfriend. He'd never even taken Caidin out in the Porsche.

For first period the next day, the principal called an assembly. Refugees were pouring into Houston, she said, and some would be enrolling at their school. A few had arrived already. At lunch they hung out in the parking lot by their souped-up cars. These didn't seem like people to be trifled with, but Caidin was lonely enough to saunter over. "How fast will that thing go?" he asked about a Charger.

"You are?"

"Caidin Maddox."

"And you drive?"

"A Porsche Carrera."

Their glances at each other seemed to say, People are the same everywhere you go. "You want to race?"

"Sure, that sounds fun," Caidin said.

"When I go fast, the cops stop me."

"So you don't want to?"

"What rules do you propose?"

"Forget it," he said, and headed to Astrid's, where she and Izzy lay on her bed packing a bong. "How was school," mocked Izzy; "what did you learn?"

"There's these refugees from Katrina."

"God knows what percentile."

When they laughed, he couldn't tell if it was at the refugees or at him. "They can have our textbooks," Astrid said. "We're joining the Rainbow Gathering."

"Then they can have mine too."

She sat up and kissed him. "We didn't think you'd come."

"Why not," he said, knowing none of them would be joining a thing.

His mood improved when Hank showed up with some ecstasy. Soon he could feel an intense, beautiful love for Astrid and everyone rolling across his shoulders. He apologized for going to school. "Let's bet on when my folks realize I've dropped out," he said, and Izzy bet next week and Hank October and Astrid never. The less you cared, the better you looked and the better you felt. He stared in the mirror at the bones lurking under his skin, trying to watch the concern dissolve away.

"I bet my eighteenth birthday," he said, "when they learn that I've become ineligible for the Air Force."

"I want go on a drive," Izzy said, which sounded great, but Hank and Astrid only stared up from the bed.

"Get in," he told Izzy, and aimed the two of them fast as ever toward the distant thunderheads. "You don't love Astrid," Izzy said while they raced across endless ranchland, "and I don't love Hank. Let's go to Bozeman."

Afraid she was about to profess her love for him, Caidin said, "Bozeman?"

"Milo's parents moved there when he died. I can't find their number, so I figured we'll just show up."

Recalling her report of Juaco's kiss—it had been amazing—he said, "How would you know who I don't love?"

"Chill out; let's have fun. Have you done salvia?"

She got a pipe out and packed it with what looked like parsley. "It's legal," she said; "it makes you high for thirty seconds."

With a finger she covered the carb. He pulled smoke in and inhaled. The highway narrowed and then faded away. It was dark now, and he was climbing the outer wall of a skyscraper, high above an abyss. He'd nearly reached the top, but his fingers didn't have much glue left. Soon he was gripping for dear life in that frigid wind. Across the glass, inside, stood his parents and all the people he'd ever called his friends. Cozily warm, they chatted together by a fire. "Let me in," he cried, but only a few even turned to watch him run out of glue and fall.

He came to in a world upside down: water for grass, dirt for sky, a herd of cattle dangling. Izzy's vomit fell up, and then he got it; he had flipped the Porsche.

They crawled out through the windows and phoned Hank.

While they waited, Caidin scraped off the vehicle ID. "Do you think God saved us?" Izzy asked.

He couldn't tell if the question was sarcastic. "I think God was trying to kill us," he said, except somehow neither he nor Izzy had suffered a scratch.

The next day he borrowed Astrid's Volvo and went to school to find there weren't seats for him in his classes. Some teachers didn't know him. Worse was when the teachers who did asked no questions about where he'd been.

"Hey," said Jeff in the lunch line.

"Sorry for skipping so much school."

"You think it harmed me?"

"Jeff, come on."

"Come on what, be your friend so I can die in a wreck?"

"How'd you hear about my wreck?"

"You had a wreck?"

"You said you'd heard."

"Was it the Porsche?"

"I didn't wreck. Screw you."

After school, instead of returning the Volvo to Astrid's, he took it home. "Where's your brother's car?" said his father, back from Dallas.

"My girlfriend's got it. This is her car."

"That's who you've been spending so much time with?"

"Yeah, I think I really like her."

"Good for you, kiddo. Good for you."

He erased Astrid's voicemail without listening to it. The next day, hoping to put things back on track, he drove to school in her car again. It was too late for the Ivy League, but in Texas the top ten percent of each class got into UT. Probably too late for that too, but he could try. On a precalculus test he scored a ninety.

"You skipped that unit, cheater," Adam said afterward.

"I'd never cheat," Caidin said, his feelings hurt. You're jealous of how hot girls like me, he thought, running a hand through his long hair.

"There's a new hurricane."

"Hadn't heard."

"I doubt your new friends watch the news."

At home that afternoon his parents had the weather on. The storm was a category three, named Rita. "This isn't some Ninth Ward shack," his mom said, but the next morning Rita had strengthened to four and it was time to leave. By midday, as school closed early, the roads were gridlocked. Ten minutes and Caidin hadn't gone half a mile. The drivers seemed like a parade of idiots for moving so slowly. He tried something new: at every intersection, if traffic was bumper-to-bumper in one direction, he chose the empty way. Soon he was far from his house, on a street he realized led past Milo Hux's neighborhood.

Knowing that they had gone, Caidin could allow a conversation with the Huxes to play out in his mind. He could even turn onto their street and drive to their gate. It was all my fault, he was telling Mr. and Mrs. Hux when he saw a man—no, a boy, tall and slender, with toffee-colored arms—standing in their front yard.

The speedometer didn't stop at 120; it went all the way to 180, yet Caidin found himself braking, lowering the window, and saying, "What are you doing?"

"Looking for somebody," said Juaco Luna, meeting Caidin's eyes. He knows, Caidin thought.

"They moved to Montana, in the Rockies."

"Yeah, I know where Montana is."

"I mean, I don't know the states of Honduras."

"El Salvador. I grew up here."

"Milo crashed his car and died."

"Yep, that's pretty much why they left town."

Juaco's lips seemed designed to look mired in a painful, constant memory, and Caidin longed to touch them.

"Why does everyone think you're Honduran?"

"That was maybe just the guy who turned me in."

Now his heart gulped blood the way his lungs gulped air. "Where's the LeBaron?" he asked, hoping it wasn't the car Milo had died in.

"Impounded."

"I'll drive you to pick it up."

"I've heard how you drive," Juaco said, but he got in.

Gripping the wheel to still his shaking arms, Caidin took them slowly forward. "Who told you about my driving?"

"Milo. He had a crush on you."

"Give me a break," Caidin said, but then he thought back on Milo's gaze in the mirror. He remembered holding Milo underwater by the shoulders, pressing down with flat palms to maximize the amount of skin he touched. Maybe he'd have strangled the boy if it meant getting to touch him.

"Milo could be kind of a bitch," Juaco said, putting a hand miraculously on Caidin's leg. "I mean I get why you teased him."

Caidin lifted his foot from the gas. On a leafy boulevard, the city skyline girding itself against roiling clouds ahead, they coasted to a halt. "Izzy Baxter says you're coming back for her," he said, trying to understand.

"Izzy's cute, but she's a total pothead."

"Why were you living at Milo's?"

"Yeah, his parents helped mine a long time ago," said Juaco, leaning over the gear shift toward Caidin.

Juaco's lips closed around Caidin's lower lip. Their tongues touched. Already Caidin was dreading the end, wishing he could freeze time. He squeezed Juaco, pulling him closer. Juaco's warm breath spread through him along every axon until he was trembling everywhere. Cars were passing; he didn't care. He hoped they saw. It occurred to him that he was cheating on Astrid, and even that felt good.

A tractor trailer sped by, the wake shaking the two of them in tandem until Juaco sat upright and touched Caidin's cheek. Only then did Caidin realize he was crying.

"You're a good-looking guy," Juaco said, drying his tear; "you'll find someone."

"I doubt I'll live that long," he said as he tried to get hold of himself.

"Don't be dumb. Everyone hates high school."

"You know there's a big hurricane."

Juaco nodded. "Yeah, I'll find a ride out of town."

"No, I'm taking you to your car," Caidin said, moving forward again, but not for long; the impound lot turned out to be ten miles toward the coast, on a highway under contraflow.

Through a twisting labyrinth of oak-lined streets he found a back route home, where his dad was on a ladder nailing boards to the windows. In the kitchen his mom was throwing out food. "This is Juaco, and he's spending the night," Caidin told her.

She narrowed her eyes. "Is Juaco a common name?"

Caidin remembered the newsletter from back in the spring. "Geez, Mom, make your own friends, okay?"

"What zone are you in?" she asked their guest. The Maddoxes' zone would depart in the morning.

"My parents already left," Juaco said, as Caidin spoke over him: "He's going tomorrow with his aunt."

Leading Juaco upstairs, a finger hovering behind the small of Juaco's back, Caidin rehearsed in his mind for the next kiss. In his bedroom, though, the mood seemed to have changed. Juaco sat down on the desk chair instead of the bed.

"How'd you get back?" Caidin said. "Did you pay a coyote?"

Juaco giggled. "This rich guy got me a visa."

"Oh." He wondered if Juaco could hear his ears' thrumming. "If we could make it to the impound lot, I've got my mom's credit card."

"Why would you do that?"

"Because I want to."

"Do you think hot people are better than regular people?"

"I just, you can't get by here without a car," Caidin said, except of course the city was being destroyed anyway.

The phone rang. "Why haven't you left, Snot?" said his brother Caleb, on the other side of the world.

"Tomorrow morning. Are you okay?"

"I'm the only guy from Houston whose folks haven't left," Caleb said, sounding more petulant than concerned.

Caidin listened to the whistling emptiness of the Iraqi steppe. "Are you the only one whose dad bribed him to go to war?" he heard himself say.

"Don't talk about Dad that way," Caleb said.

"I wrecked the Porsche," he said, suddenly wanting to hurt his brother. "I was high. It's probably totaled."

"You've always been a shitty liar."

"Seriously, who tries so hard to send his sons to war?"

"Who talks about his dad that way?"

Before Caidin could answer exactly who, the dial tone began to hum.

"Will your dad bribe you too?" Juaco asked.

"It was more of a threat than a bribe," Caidin said. "But it only works if you care whether he's ashamed."

They played Xbox awhile, and then they watched the evacuation. When Juaco fell asleep on Caidin's bed, Caidin muted the TV and watched him instead. Just barely, he let his finger brush against the tiny hairs on Juaco's arm. Of course hot people are better, he was thinking when the knocks came, in the blast-beat pattern of the *Poisoned Wasteland* theme music.

The door swung open, the light came on. "I need my games," said Jeff. "We're leaving in an hour for. . . . Oh."

Juaco opened his eyes. "Are you Jeff?"

"My folks are waiting," said Jeff, ejecting a cartridge from the console.

"If you're Jeff, Milo thanks you for being nice."

Meticulously looking away from the bed, Jeff took another game from the shelf. Say something, Caidin thought. Say I saw you touching Juaco just now. Say dead people can't give thanks. Say dude, the kid you're lying next to killed your friend. But Jeff said only, "Hope you booked a hotel."

"Mom's friends with the whole capitol," Caidin said. "We'll probably sleep in the governor's spare rooms."

Jeff turned out the light and closed the door behind him. Soon Juaco was snoring again, and Caidin lay awake wondering who else Milo had left messages for. Was there one for Caidin, too hatefully worded for Juaco to show him? Or had Juaco deemed the message too kind? He might never know. He fell asleep and awoke to a ringing phone. "Put Cleo in her carrier," his mother said. "We're almost home."

Outside, wind was whipping the live oaks. To the east the sky was ash-gray, while an otherworldly green light shone in the west. "Juaco's coming with us," he said.

"Get dressed, Caidin. They've raised it to five."

"You'd rescue a cat and not my friend?"

"You told me his aunt?"

"There's no aunt. He came back alone to get the automatic scholarship." Instantly Caidin knew his guess must be a correct one: their school was the best in Texas, and Juaco was at the top of their class. Juaco hadn't returned for Milo, Izzy, Caidin, or anyone but himself.

Just as quickly, Caidin realized how dumb it was to think so, when it was at school that Juaco had been exposed.

"Cleo's part of our family. Your friend has a family. Now where's the Porsche?"

"I got high on salvia and flipped it."

"We need it in the garage!"

"Most likely it's already at a garage. After I go surfing, I'll call around."

Juaco was up and putting on his shoes. "We're taking the Volvo," Caidin told him. "We'll meet up with my folks in Austin."

"Dude. Is that even your car?"

"No, it's my girlfriend's. Come on."

Juaco crossed the room, turned to study Caiden. "Best of luck," he said, and he headed for the stairs.

Caidin followed him down. "I mean, where else would you go? San Salvador?"

"Not to hurt your feelings, but I'd rather live in Fallujah than stay with your folks."

Juaco had reached the landing. Behind him, Caidin grasped for any threat or promise that would stop him from exiting into the gale. He thought Juaco must have seen what unreturned love had done to Milo, and yesterday's kiss was his revenge. It was a plan so elegantly cruel that Caidin wondered what percentile Juaco had scored on the IQ test. Separate from his withering heart was a sudden dread that his parents' maid, Consuela, might be approaching the door as Juaco opened it. She wasn't. He walked out, and dwindled into the shower of lantana flowers and air plants. What a stupid thing to have feared. So was the entire storm. Rita could destroy Houston for all Caidin cared, because aside from this, nothing was ever going to go wrong.

GAINLINESS

VICTOR WAS A PECULIAR BOY, said his parents' few friends, an assessment that irked Victor even as he suspected it was correct. Take his cage dream. Lying awake nights, he fancied himself shackled to a wall beside the home-schooled boys from across the road. A hook-nosed villain would poke him and those boys with a pitchfork, naked. If he felt himself falling asleep during this fantasy, he pressed ice to his face to sustain the scene. What was this if not peculiar? He carried needle-nose pliers in his pocket for extracting snot without touching it. Journeys of any length had to begin on his left foot. He peed sitting down. After brushing his teeth he swallowed the toothpaste, risky as that might be, because he'd always done it that way.

In 1985, when Victor was seven, a friend of his mother's came to visit Yazoo City. This spice-scented, easy-mannered fellow, who had the mellifluous name of Micah, said to Victor, "You're trouble."

"Don't," said Victor's mother, but Micah went on: "It's true. When you're older, Victor, you'll be a truckload of trouble."

Something stirred in Victor to hear it, but he kept quiet. Later, after Micah had gone, Victor found his mother weeping in the kitchen. "I won't be trouble," he said to her.

"Micah's telling people bye is why I'm crying."

"What's wrong with that?"

"I mean he's sick."

"I'm sorry," Victor could have replied, or "Why," but instead he said, "Micah's a name I wouldn't hate."

"You can change your name when you're grown." They'd been through this already. To base his favor on the sound of names was another quirk of Victor's. If he were, say, a Micah, hearing tell of a Victor, he would hate that boy's guts—not because Victor meant *winner* but because the name's ugly asymmetry suggested an ungainly boy. It disappointed his parents, Mary and Ralph, for him to feel this way. But theirs were neutral names. Victor didn't adore one or hate the other, the way he did with Albert and Sievert Alfsson across the road.

Albert and Sievert were twins with identically curly manes of yellow hair, but from Victor's bedroom window perch he could distinguish them readily. Albert was chubby, for one, but more importantly Victor's grandfather had been an Albert. The name connoted decrepitude, unsightliness. He'd never known a Sievert, on the other hand. Sievert—impish, lithe, fresh—was the only twin Victor yearned to touch. If asked what sounded nice about the boy's name, he couldn't have answered. Why were bluebirds pretty? Self-evident. The problem started when Sievert quit coming outside.

For months he showed up only in the back of the Alfssons' station wagon as Mrs. Alfsson drove out of the garage. Out his window Victor would watch roly-poly Albert bouncing alone on a pogo stick, thousands of times in a row.

"Is Micah dead yet?" he asked his mother one day, thinking that in her grief she might rename him after her late friend.

"I'm sick of your crap, Victor," she replied, upsetting him so much that he quit breathing. His skin tingled, his sight blackened, and he passed out cold. He awoke to find Mary pressing a cold cloth to his forehead.

"Thank God," she said, as if she'd solved the problem and not caused it.

Lying there under her pressed washcloth, Victor said, "Where am I?" He wanted to freak her out, because he was hurt by the betrayal of her words. It was more than their sentiment—it was that *crap*, ugly in both sound and meaning, smack at the end of a blame. A voiceless bilabial stop, as vexing as the voiceless velar plosive at the end of his father's favorite word. Although he couldn't analyze consonants that way yet, he knew what he didn't like. He breathed more quickly, aware of sucking in air, of being a breathing body. When his lungs filled up, would he remember to quit? Could he turn things around? Maybe not. His skin tingled, his sight vanished. Again he was gone.

After a dozen more such spells Ralph suggested specialists, like a pediatric cardiologist, whereas Mary suggested that Victor buck up. "He needs to act like a grown-up," she said to Ralph, who went behind Mary's back to find a shrink named Dolf Pappadopolous.

"I doubt your son will ever feel a normal range of emotions," said Dr. Pappadopolous to Ralph as Victor sat between them. "This will worsen at puberty. His grasp of metaphor will be impeded, if it develops at all."

"What kind of name is your name?" said Victor, phrasing the query so as not to utter any of its horrid mishmash.

"Greek and German. You probably have not heard of a Dolf, but go to West Germany, you will meet more." Dr. Pappadopolous might as well have said, "Dunk your head in the toilet, you will eat a turd." Victor's head grew light again, his vision clouded. He put a hand out to steady himself.

"He does it again, you see? Makes himself faint? You or I could decide not to, but that is the nature of the dilemma."

If he was fainting on purpose, Victor thought, he should faint again now. If some illness was causing his problem, he should remain awake. Which action would prove this odious man wrong? He breathed sharply in and out, considering the question. Before he could choose, his lungs ballooned so full of air that he panicked again and it was too late already. He awakened on the table as Ralph pleaded, "Son?"

Victor didn't mean to reply with silence. He just didn't know what to say. It wasn't the names themselves so much as how no one, not even Ralph, perceived why Victor responded negatively. The answer wasn't as simple as a need for aesthetic bliss. In his dungeon dream the sole color was the dull gray of concrete, of cinder blocks, of skin gone sallow in lantern light. There wasn't electricity. It wasn't the 1980s above that cellar maze, but a timeless realm without paved roads or child safety laws. The master of a lush, unspoiled land had banished each ugly thing underground, where Victor sat chained to a ball. How could he explain to his anxious father that he didn't miss the sun? In an airy meadow overhead, wisps danced in the light, while Victor basked in the well-being he drew from knowing that all was neatly fenced off by the planet's curve: grandeur above, everything else below.

As time passed, the quarrels over Victor's bouts grew bigger. Ralph moved out, out of Yazoo City entirely, into an apartment in Hattiesburg. After that the house stayed messier. Alone with his mother, Victor learned to steady himself through fussy tidying. For an hour each evening he wiped down surfaces, straightened things just so. Out in the world, he and Mary would take the old highway past pawn shops, auto garages, the ball fields where several strata of asphalt merged in a chaotic pimple of broken tarmac. Victor suspected that none of the Little Leaguers hyperventilated, as he did, at the sight of Queen Anne's lace sprouting through those pavement cracks. He alone hung a wrecking ball from space to demolish every derelict building as they passed. By shutting his left eye, he crushed whatever needed it on that side, likewise with his other eye on the right. He was uncompromising. Whole cities he flattened while imagining them from a bird's-eye view, like the hideously named Hattiesburg, and then he seeded the scars with tulip bulbs, and that was how it was for years, until the day in ninth grade when he spotted Sievert Alfsson mowing the Alfssons' lawn, a breeze rippling his open shirt and blonde curls.

Transfixed, Victor knelt at the window. He'd never seen such a compelling boy before, or a richer contrast between someone's ruddy skin and the green grass. For half an hour Sievert mowed. When he was done, he leaned on the lawnmower handle and gazed toward Victor's house until Victor raised a hand.

Sievert did the same, in a gesture that could only mean he was beckoning Victor to come say hello.

Heart fluttering, Victor ventured outside on his left foot. He crossed into the Alfssons' yard and ended in front of his neighbor on his right foot.

"Hey, Victor," said Sievert in a voice whose deep pitch stirred Victor and rendered him briefly mute.

"I'm Micah," he finally managed to reply.

"I thought you're Victor."

"That's my middle name."

"My dad says you're disturbed."

"My mom says you're a Seventh-Day Adventist."

"Sievert's one, but I worship the devil."

Victor's impulse was to correct this boy: "Sievert's you," he nearly said, but in fact he was speaking to ugly old Albert.

He looked the alleged Albert up and down, judging whether this newly slim kid could own such a hideous name. "You're skinny," he said, his lungs seizing a little.

"So?" said Albert, as if it had been ever thus.

"How do you worship the devil?"

"You drink," Albert said, pulling out a flask.

Albert sipped, then passed the flask to Victor, who took it, stealing a glance across the road. He'd done nothing like this before. Albert was home-schooled, ignorant of Victor's reputation as a good kid.

I'm Micah, he thought, tilting the flask to his lips to pour what tasted like medicine into his mouth. Immediately he could feel stamina spreading through him, coating his insides as he choked on the burn.

"Too hot for a shirt," said Albert, pulling his own off to toss it at his feet.

It was only about sixty degrees out, with cool gusts of wind. "Yeah," Victor said.

"Been in the woods?"

"Those?" said Victor, gesturing behind the Alfssons'.

"Know some others?" retorted Albert, so that Victor heard how moronic he'd just sounded. Did he always sound that way? He fell out of the moment and stood thinking of Albert's name, his grandpa Albert, wizened old men, until a tingling moved up his arms. Once again he would faint unless he did something. Albert was now squeezing under a barbed-wire fence toward a stand of pines. In alarm Victor drank. Right away, something flowed through him again and halted his decline. A layer of dry needles softened the pine-cone crunch under his feet as Victor hurried into the dark of the woods.

"My dad works for the radio," Albert said when Victor had caught up, "so there's free trips to Gulf Shores. What's yours do?"

"He moved out of town."

"Where'd he move?"

"East of here." Victor didn't want to say *Hattiesburg.*

"My mom's on disability. She's possessed."

"Mine's a nurse."

"She wrote to Rome to ask for an exorcist, but they wouldn't send one, so she switched to Adventist."

"Mine's nothing," said Victor, giggling, because the alcohol was in his blood now, and his body felt like an unclenching fist.

"Here's the swamp."

They emerged into a meadow where willows grew by the shore of a cow pond. It wasn't a swamp. From now on, thought Victor as he drank again, if he felt like saying something dumb like "It's not a swamp," he would drink instead.

"Dad will whip me later," said Albert with a cramped smile.

"He won't find out," said Victor.

"Maybe I want it," said Albert, and suddenly it didn't matter if the blonde fuzz on Albert's arm belonged to someone with an unattractive name; Victor couldn't go any longer without touching it. He reached a hand tentatively toward the boy. It felt like he was pushing through a thick morass. Then, as his finger hovered near Albert's skin, a heron's wings flapped, rippling the water.

Scared out of his reverie, Victor pulled back. "I wanted it to keep going," said Albert, as if he meant the approach of Victor's hand.

"Getting whipped?"

"Sievert and I punch each other."

Following his new protocol Victor sipped from the flask until he had a better reply than "I like Sievert's name." The better one was, "Why?"

"To see who can take more hits."

"Should I do it to you?"

"Are you gay?"

"You just said you like it."

"No, assmunch."

"Want to do it to me?"

"In the face like a girl?"

"However you like," said Victor, immediately gulping down an impulse to take it back, to run away from this strange thrall. He folded his hands across his lap. Beyond Albert the sky was ripe with white clouds that floated above the pines while Albert's cupped palm whooshed in to slap him. Right away Albert gasped as if he'd been the one hit.

"Happy now?" he asked.

"I guess," said Victor, his cheek stinging.

"Again, assmunch?" said Albert, as Victor kept unclenching. Hard not to conflate that with the stinging, so he presented his cheek. He breathed with ease. He hadn't liked the slap, but being drunk felt sublime. His lungs weren't tight anymore. His head didn't hurt. He had binocular vision, not just in the merging of his two eyes' fields but in the two halves of the earth. In this new state as he awaited Albert's palm, beauty wasn't repelling ugliness. He desired no stick for raking scum off the pond water. He didn't care about the trash strewn on the far shore.

From then on, Albert let Victor drink with him once a week when his family was at service. They did it in Albert's basement and in the woods, in an abandoned school bus there, or by the pond where it had first happened. A summer evening in the school bus could calm Victor for a week. They smoked Marlboros Albert purchased from the cousin who sold him gin. They arrived home reeking of gin and cigarettes, so Victor started stowing a toothbrush and toothpaste behind a loose house brick, brushing his teeth to mask the scent. Not that Mary noticed stuff like that. As for Albert, he didn't care what his parents smelled; he hated them for messing up his brother's head.

"What did they do to it?" asked Victor more than once, to which Albert would say only, "Fucked it up."

Victor hadn't forgotten how he used to react to the harsh edges at the end of *fuck* and *crap*. Such a childish kid he'd been. "Is that why you worship the devil?"

"Micah, don't be a dipshit."

"What do you mean?"

"Should I hit you again?"

Victor nodded not because he liked the feeling, but because of symmetry. If Albert wished to slap him, and Victor wished to allow it, there was symmetry. Anyway it never hurt much, at least not until the day Albert watched him brush his teeth.

They had spent three hours in the bus. Afterward Victor swallowed the toothpaste like usual.

"Raise your arms," Albert said then. When Victor did, Albert punched him in the gut. He dropped his toothbrush and bowled over.

"Why'd you do that?" he howled.

"Because you're retarded."

"For swallowing toothpaste?"

"Did you swallow toothpaste?"

"I've always done it that way."

"You're worse than Sievert," said Albert, turning to go.

As he crossed the road home, the curtains fluttered in the Alfssons' living room. "I don't care," said Victor aloud, enjoying the words as he spoke them. He stayed put afterward, admiring their echo. Nothing was symmetrical about *I don't care*, but the phrase wasn't ungainly. He was seeing beyond its shape and sound to the deeper meaning, the notion of not caring. Who gives a fuck, he thought, feeling wise beyond his years. That night, still buzzed, he spat his toothpaste out for the first time. Thinking back to Albert's last withering glance he watched it swirl down the drain.

The next morning, sober but still wise, he did the same. "It's what I always do," he let himself whisper aloud, a workman-like phrase striking in its plainness. After a few more days, spitting was old hat. The shift proved so strangely easy that, when Albert didn't show up the following weekend at the usual hour, Victor braved beginning a journey on his right foot, ending on the Alfssons' porch on his left.

He rang the bell. Almost immediately the door opened to reveal white-haired Mr. Alfsson, his hazel cat-eyes daring Victor to ask, "Albert home?"

"Where Albert is is the Lyman Ward Military Academy," Mr. Alfsson said. "You can write to him there."

"When will he be back?"

"Sievert is inside. Would you like to play with Sievert?"

"Okay," he heard himself say, but he meant *no*. Suddenly Sievert appeared at the top of the stairs, as fat as his brother used to be. Their spirits had traded bodies, Victor thought, already pondering an excuse to leave. "I forgot my mother needs me," he said, backing away.

Switching feet hadn't worked out, he thought as he headed home. He should obey his own rules, heed words' sounds and keep things tidy, swallow his toothpaste every time. Except he was realizing something. He wasn't sad to lose Albert. Or he detected no sadness. What he gulped down as he crept across the road was excitement. Adrenaline. At school there were tons of better-looking boys than Albert, with names as hideous as Hugh and Horace and he didn't care, he had put that crap behind him. Names were subjective. The objective problem was obtaining alcohol.

Victor studied that problem until the day a Desert Storm veteran and addict in recovery came to speak at Magnolia High. On the gym bleachers, Victor positioned himself behind two kids he'd heard speaking on the subject in biology class, the ugly-named Hugh and Hugh's neutral-named friend Clint. It seemed they drank from Clint's parents' liquor cabinet while they played Dungeons & Dragons. The fact that they were gaming nerds lowered the stakes for Victor, who waited to make his move until the assembly speaker alleged that no one ever wanted to grow up and become a drunk.

"I want to grow up and become a drunk ASAP," Victor said.

Hugh laughed and turned to see who'd spoken.

"I'll be better at it," Victor added. "I'll set high goals."

They got to talking. Victor mentioned Dungeons & Dragons admiringly. Soon enough Hugh was suggesting he hang out with them. Did he want to? "Why not," Victor answered. Within hours they were in Clint's bedroom pouring peach schnapps and rolling dice to learn what qualities his character would have in the campaign.

For six months Victor played D&D, drinking more than Hugh and Clint and their other friends. The fakeness of the game's dungeons compared to his dungeons stopped mattering. The energy he'd once spent hating names like Hugh's he funneled into a crush on the boy, battling orcs until finally he acknowledged that they would never get naked together. That didn't stymie him long. He drank until his old idiosyncrasies were like a logic problem he'd solved. He started going to the quarry on weekends. One moonlit Friday there, as some girls teased him about his gaming days, he thought how lucky he was that the Alfssons had banished Albert. Without outgrowing Albert, he couldn't have outgrown Hugh. Now he would also outgrow these girls, along with their friends. It was a destiny that seemed to stem from innate willpower. Night after night he drank with whomever at whatever house, whatever their names. Then one day as he was about to check the mailbox, he heard someone saying, "Micah," and gazed across at a gigantic figure in the Alfssons' downstairs window, summoning him.

Ignore, pretend, thought Victor. In a sort of trance, he walked over. There in a window that rose to the level of his neck, backward on a couch, knelt a curly-haired teenager bloated to nearly three hundred pounds.

For a moment Victor feared there'd been yet another spirit trade, until the pale, obese boy said, "I need to discuss Albert."

"You're supposed to be in high school," Victor said, hoping none of his friends would drive past and see.

"I'm in the equivalent of the twentieth grade. It's Albert who's unwell."

"Come again?" said Victor, although he'd heard clearly.

"He wonders why you abandoned him."

When Victor didn't answer, Sievert carried on. "He sends you love letters that our mom burns. He carved your name in his bed frame and everyone saw."

"I'm sorry."

"You've never asked for his address."

"What's his address?"

"If you don't love Albert back, write it. I'll send it."

Through the window Sievert offered a sheet of paper, the

sight of whose untidy torn chads made Victor yearn for a drink.
"Why would you want his heart broken?" he asked.

"If he falls out of love, he won't go to hell."

"Okay," said Victor, taking the paper along with a pen.
Against the house siding he wrote, *Dear Albert.* About to tell a
vague lie like *I miss you*, he wondered what kind of retard carved
into a bed that he loved a boy.

He glanced behind him at his own house and imagined Sievert
peering through a telescope, jacking off and eating hot dogs.

Fat Sievert was the one who loved him.

Now Victor knew exactly what to do. *I have a whole new life*,
he wrote on the paper. *We were immature kids. You called yourself
a devil worshiper, which is stupid. I don't miss you. I never loved you.*
—*Victor (Micah)*

"Here," he said, handing it back.

"Thanks," said Sievert. "Bye."

Retreating across the Alfssons' yard, Victor doubted his reasoning. If Sievert really liked him, he'd have kept him lingering
longer by the window. "Wait!" he would be calling. And what if
he mailed the letter? Walking faster, Victor grew light-headed the
way he used to. The idea of a lovelorn Albert reading his hateful
words might have sent him regressing into a panic if not for the
acceptance packet he discovered in the mailbox from Tulane.

Disrobing in his bedroom before the open blinds, Victor
recalled his idea that Sievert was a hot name. It wasn't. Nor was
it a fat name. Names, like most things, were far more complicated
than that. He'd been correct to deem the world half beautiful and
half ugly, but he'd been wrong to seek a clear dividing line. The
correct line split past from future. His task as a curator of aesthetic
pleasure was to locate ugliness in the future, and sequester it in
the past. He'd done as much with Albert and Sievert, and now he

would do it with Mississippi, too. To tidy the world in this way gratified him. Buzzing with expectancy, he knelt. As he touched himself in sight of the Alfssons' family room, he allowed himself one last image of his old friend in his defaced cot at military school, weeping poignantly for Victor, unaware of falling into the past.

Victor's cocaine habit began the night he arrived in New Orleans, when he asked an upperclassman in the dorm to point him toward the gay bars. A cab took him to Bourbon Street, where a spot called Oz swarmed with celebrants of something called Southern Decadence. Victor wound up on a balcony among men thrice his age. "Looks like trouble," said one. "Truckload," said another, bringing Victor's rigid childhood mind clamping down on him. But before he could explore his panic's source, someone bought him a whiskey. His need to demand that these drunks be annihilated along with their gaudy city vanished like any flash of déjà vu. Where had he been all their lives? Did he want to come into the bathroom? Yes, he replied, and yes to all that was asked on every sultry evening from there on out. The flirters would muss his hair, smiling at their sly prowess as if he might ever tell anyone no. He didn't.

Years passed. He liked how New Orleans had so few unsightly buildings. The ones that did exist never had him gasping for breath. He considered structural design often enough that he wound up majoring in it, then entering the master's program. He thought too about the design of his face. Men were asking if he'd considered modeling. No, he replied coyly each time, as if he had no idea of his effect on people. He'd been drinking enough to rarely eat. Was it conceited to believe the svelte angles of his jaw derived from his state of mind? With his clutter of tics, he'd been an ugly child. These days he barely had to slouch against a bar before someone touched him.

During hangovers a memory would surface of his writing *I don't miss you, I never loved you,* and he would bury his face in his hands. Mostly, though, he was drunk and high.

In his second year of grad school he never got around to applying for internships, but it didn't matter, a partner at a prestigious firm fell for him at a bar. Victor had been staring at this silver fox's wing-tipped shoes when the man said, "Salvatore Ferragamo."

At first that seemed to be Gary's name. "I'm Victor," he replied.

"You're the sort of boy folks like to take advantage of."

"What do you mean?" he said, sensing already the pheromones Gary was exuding as he fell in love. The capture was as easy as that. A string of endless hot days followed, during which Victor seemed to have stumbled into his own dream-life. Gary lived in a mansion full of mirrors and varnished wood, where old-guard fetishists whiled away their dissolute days in high abandon. Bolted to the bedroom wall was a barred-top pup cage Gary would padlock him inside of. I've arrived, thought Victor, soaking naked with the guys in a backyard pool, nursing hangovers with mint juleps. Reasoning that Gary would give him a job whenever he asked, he felt no urgency to start work. Soon a dozen coke dealers knew his name, which filled him with well-being akin to professional pride. He would emerge from blackouts inhaling powder off Gary's house key. "Boys have committed suicide over me," he told the barflies who had become his friends. "I was fourteen when I got one sent off to military school."

"You must have been a hot fourteen-year-old."

"Albert thought so," he said with a curt laugh. "When I arrived to bust him out, he'd already slit his wrists."

"Did you love him?"

"I lived to see another day."

Chuckling again, Victor wondered if his letter might really have pushed Albert over the edge. Later, alone, he searched online for his old friend. None of the Albert Alfssons he found was the one he'd known. A quest for Sievert led him to a blog about the complexity of God, with no photograph or mention of family. If he phoned home to Mississippi, his mother would inquire about his work. He'd lie and tell her he had a job. Best not to call again until it became true.

One evening in January Gary kicked him out. In a near blackout Victor walked to the antique shop run by a man who winked at him in bars. His name was Ernest, and he moonlighted as a fashion photographer. "Of course I want you," he said, so Victor spent the next days modeling for Ernest under vaulted ceilings replete with metal leaf. Ernest's lurid stories of the merchant marine took place in every port from Manila to Marseilles. Victor listened carefully, planning to retell them as if they were his. For months, whenever he finished a bottle of scotch, Ernest would replace it. One humid day he overheard Ernest telling the phone, "Keep your hands off him if you know what's good," so it came as a surprise when he too banished Victor, kicking him out into the Marigny. But there were plenty of antique shops a boy like Victor could choose from.

Victor lived with James. He lived with Phillip. He lived with Ian and Timothy and Rufus. For short stints he worked as a waiter at high-end restaurants, intending to begin real work when he felt like it. He lived with Leroy, Bruce, Sebastian. Two bars banned him in one night. He developed prediabetes. He got his own apartment. The more fun he had, the more he blacked out. His cheeks grew gin blossoms. Hours after his aunt phoned to say his mother had died of ovarian cancer, he awoke without memory of that conversation. Sure, a foreboding anxiety gripped him, but that was typical of the hours prior to a first drink. He went to the Eagle and got wasted on hurricanes. In the darkroom he met a Cajun named Thierry and rode with him out to a fishing cabin on Bayou Dupont. That was where he smoked crystal for the first time. Time increased to lightning speed under phase after phase of the moon. At some point, convinced the pelicans floating on black water were spy cameras, he left for home, and crossed into the Sprint service area to discover the voicemails.

Soaking in a hot bath, Victor steeled himself to explain that he'd been away on an architectural commission in Central America. He was already so sober that he could hardly imagine speaking at all, let alone telling and then maintaining a complex lie. He'd missed the funeral anyway. Why bother, he thought as the water grew cold. He pulled up his aunt in his phone contacts and deleted the number. Then he collected the liquor bottles from every room and poured them out in the sink.

Late on that first sober day the liquid in him began trickling into his fingers to evaporate into the stale air. That was why his hands quivered the way they did. Soon his head throbbed, too, because his brain was bouncing around in the newly desiccated space. By sunset he was hallucinating that his couch was an exam table. On a nearby table lay his cancerous mother, awaiting news of who would live and who would not. He clenched his fists and kicked and turned, the ringing phone pitching him into further visions where Mary hung shackled to that wall he'd dreamt. Her presence there rendered the place horrific, a torture chamber, which he supposed it had always been. Desperate to be helped, he gripped the phone, but everyone fell into three untenable categories: alcoholics, relatives, and ex-boyfriends. He powered it off and watched a spy movie. After that one, another. During a commercial for beds, his shakes gave way to something worse.

"Tchoupitoulas Mattress Madness at Chuck's Tchoupitoulas Mattress at 5300 Tchoupitoulas," shouted the TV.

Hearing that garishly unparallel name repeated, Victor thought he might be suffering a heart attack. His breath tightened. It was as if he hadn't outgrown his attacks at all. Then, as the man bellowed it all again, the ghastly, elegant truth struck Victor. Although he'd lived half his life near Tchoupitoulas Street, he'd always been drunk.

Half in nightmare already, he barely noticed his brain shutting off. He passed out cold. The next morning he awoke into a period he would think back on as a new, outsized childhood. Looking around at the squalor of his basement apartment he saw cobwebs in the corners, piles of garments, cluttered trash. He couldn't take it; he shut his eyes again until he was too parched to lie still. He stood up to find water. Landing on his right foot, he stopped, sat down, rose again on the other side.

"Just a test," he said aloud, as if his mother now spectated in heaven. He made a point of arriving on his right foot at the sink.

He gulped water and promised himself to clean the apartment, but as he scanned the room he saw there would be no way to scrub out its sheer lopsidedness. There were low ceilings, half-windows up to the street. If he was to remain sober, he would just have to suffer through it until he found a salaried job. How to do that, though, when everywhere he turned there was only ugliness: the phlegmy French names of the avenues and neighborhoods, his unclassically proportioned apartment, the Uptown bars where whole years had dwindled away, the men who lived in them, the names of liquors—Dewar's—the name Gary, Gary's white beard, Ernest's gray one, the name Ernest, all of it so suddenly, viscerally nasty that he dreamt of a lobotomy just to soothe himself into a breath?

The prospect of AA meetings, where drunks would speak their names aloud and he would say, "I'm Victor," gave Victor such apoplexy that he cut an index card to wallet size and listed

Blackouts
Drunk nose
Prediabetic
Fat
Unemployed
Barebacking
Reflux
Credit cards
Drunk driving
Shat pants

along with three more columns of dire reminders. Whenever he felt like drinking he took the card out and read it. After a week its edges were worn and he'd spoken only to store clerks. He wondered if he could have befriended anyone, ever, without liquor's aid. Within minutes of his first drink, he'd made a first friend, and all other friends had derived from that one. There'd been a domino effect, he was thinking when a FedEx man arrived with an envelope from a Yazoo City probate court.

Of course, thought Victor as he tore into it: he was his mother's next of kin. He skimmed through reams of papers. He would inherit the house, sell it, live off the income. Everything happens for a reason, he was telling himself when he read the executor's name.

Now he fell into a vision. On the body of a strapping teenage Albert Alfsson, Victor saw a rheumy-eyed and hoary head. Floating near it was a disembodied hand, slapping him. He let the papers fall, and sat down. It wasn't a pleasant vision. The quality of his sight was deteriorating, along with the fantasy itself. The old parts aged, the youthful ones regressed. Soon he beheld the aged infant Albert in the air before him. He didn't faint, though. He sat still until his legs went to sleep. Finally he collected himself enough to stand up. He collected the papers, too, threw them into the trash, carried the trash out, came in again, locked the door, lowered the blinds, and lay down.

Law & Order proved most useful: twenty seasons, five hundred hours. It had mostly neutral names, disyllabic, Scots-Irish or English. Aside from his walks to the corner for DVDs and cigarettes, he stayed home ordering delivery. He watched the spin-offs, gaining weight. He watched *The West Wing, Deadwood, 24.* When characters spoke words he didn't like, or called each other by ugly names, his breath caught, but that was better than not watching. During *Lost* he struggled to button his jeans. By *Six Feet Under* he'd stopped wearing them except on cigarette runs. On the day his Visa card quit working, he was cinching his pant waist up with his left hand.

"Got another card?" the clerk asked Victor, but his wallet was in his left pocket. His right hand held the pen, ready to sign a receipt.

"Maybe," he said, leaning against the counter. Using the pressure as a sort of belt to free up his hands, he retrieved the Discover card. It felt like a divine gift for that one to go through. He looped the grocery bag around the pants hand and headed home, smoking with his right hand until he saw a ruddy-faced blonde man by his apartment stairs. The adrenaline of recognizing Albert Alfsson felt like a hit of pure cocaine.

"You're home," Albert said. He seemed younger than he should be.

Clutching his waist, Victor approached. "Who are you?" he said, falsely.

"You seem kind of peaked."

"I've got food poisoning," said Victor, going for the stairs.

Albert followed him in as he hurried to the couch. "It's been hard to find you."

"I've been designing a museum."

"Let's get down to brass tacks. Your mom didn't have many folks caring for her. I was there a lot. I read her rites."

Victor sat on the couch. He put his head in his hands. Albert's words were fading in and out, and it was hard to follow his drift, at least until he held up a paper.

I have a whole new life, it read in Victor's loopy scrawl. *We were immature kids. I don't miss you. I never loved you.*

"This is a copy. My lawyer has the original."

"I thought Sievert was lying," said Victor, his skin clammy.

"Sievert's a Christian."

"If you kept it—"

"Your mom kept it."

"I don't understand."

"I needed Mary to explain why you'd said those things."

"Take the house," said Victor at once, as if that would cancel out a decade of his behavior. "It's yours." His fingers were tingling again. He wished Albert would hit him, slap him silly. Those fucked-up fantasies, the hook-nosed villain: his mind had known it should be punished for what he'd do. It had sought preemptive redemption, Victor thought, as his body hummed with a nearly electric vibration and silvery specks blotted out Albert's handsome face.

He awoke to Albert pressing a compress to his forehead. He'd been laid out on the couch. All these years later, blonde fuzz still dotted Albert's sinewy arms.

"Are you awake?"

"Please go away," Victor said.

"Do you want to hear her answer?"

Shaking his head, he could see movement in the far left of his vision. He had left the TV on mute. It was showing a close-up of the stricken face of Ruth Fisher, the brittle mother in *Six Feet Under*. Albert would leave, he thought with a thrill, and he could rewind the DVD and watch what was happening to Ruth.

"She said, 'A pediatric psychiatrist warned us he'd be this way.'"

Now he sat upright. "The house is yours," he said again. Albert could raise boys of his own in it, teach them the Bible, slap them. Anything to shut him up.

"She knew it's not your fault. She pitied you. She used to drive down here and watch you from across the bar."

"Albert, stop talking."

"I want to sell it on your behalf, set up a trust. Do you know what that means? A trust like Sievert's?"

That was when a wild idea grew in Victor.

"You don't even have a twin," he said. "You and Sievert are the same." Sievert had liked Victor because Sievert was Albert. Sievert had posted that letter to himself, locked himself indoors, gained weight and lost it.

"Oh, come on. Don't be stupid, Micah. You watched us play ball. We saw you every day, sticking those pliers up your nose."

"I did no such thing," said Victor, astonished to recall renaming himself after all those years. It hardly seemed real. I am Micah, he'd said over and over into the mirror, yearning to swap names with a man who had died of AIDS.

A line came into focus: the one he'd drawn to cleave the present from the past. It wasn't a line of aesthetic pleasure; it was a line of shame. Horrified by his words, his deeds, his very nature, he'd drawn a line to sequester himself from the people who loved him. Until today, it had seemed structurally viable, because no one had breached it. No one had bothered trying. He imagined a stronger one, the one Albert must have drawn across his own world. That was what people did: they drew lines across their worlds. But Albert's was a line of capability—a circle, it seemed, with Victor and Sievert trapped inside, and Albert peering across at them.

How wrong the old Yazoo City shrink turned out to have been. The swapping of names had been a metaphor all along. It was all metaphor. What was the shrink called? He let Albert's speech blur into a droning din. He exhaled. By the time the name of Dr. Dolf Pappadopolous came bursting forth, he had only to conjure his favorite gin label—*Bombay Sapphire*, words more honeyed to him sober than he'd ever noted drunk—and the spell subsided.

"Please go," he said, taking his list out of his wallet. He scanned over the ugly words, waiting for a concerned query. If Albert read the card, he might refuse to leave, well up with tears, declare his abiding love.

Here it comes, Victor was thinking, when his friend stood up and offered a hand.

"Sorry for your loss," said Albert, arm extended, reaching into the space between them until Victor laid his list down to receive a farewell shake.

BLOOD BROTHERS

I FOUND RAY UP IN the mountains at the I-40 rest stop, where I used to cruise sometimes. He was leaning against a wall, albino-pale, with these watery fish eyes. We messed around in a stall for a bit, and then he said to meet him at the red truck by the ravine.

In his truck cab he produced an uncapped light bulb. The Pigeon River roared below us. "Keeps you up," he said, "as in hard," and I yelped when it burned my fingers. He barked a joyless *heh*. We got to talking: his wife was Sheila and mine was Lisa, and his kids were Ray Junior and Angel and I don't have kids. After we were too high to talk, I guess I told him to start driving. Two days and we were in Lubbock. Now it didn't matter anymore if the bulb was hot; the burn felt good. Sometimes he'd smack me upside the head, which we both liked.

He asked what I'd do if he broke my arm.

"Go to the E.R."

"But to me."

"Break yours back?"

He nodded like it was the right answer. He knew this stuff; so did his wife, who had more sense than to do what Lisa does, which is report me missing. Six days after I'd met him we rolled back into Pigeon Forge to find the cops at my place. "Drive," Ray growled, so I did. Halfway up the mountain he held a sheath knife to my throat. "You've been filming me," he said. "I don't care if it's your wife that called; they've seen the film."

He was giving off this ugly leaden smell, and I could feel blood draining down through me, through my neck. "Thought it was you filming me, Ray."

Ray looked behind us as if back toward Texas, lowered the knife, and said, "Makes you jumpy."

"Lisa, she was the one."

"If you're a cop, you're a brave cop."

He motioned for me to face him. When I did, he put the knife to my wrist and cut it open. My yell came out as a *heh* like his laugh. He did the same to his wrist and pressed them together. He said it was a bowie knife from the Indian Wars and we were blood brothers. I said, "But what about," and the loons hollered and he said if you catch it, you get the flu, is how you know.

At his house, a log cabin, a girl was jumping rope. "Call if you get the flu," he said, but then I left without his number. Back home Lisa ran barefoot into the mud and beat her fists on my chest. "I don't know," I told her as she carried on, "I woke up an hour ago outside the hospital." Next thing I knew I was in the paper, which upset my ma. When I was twelve, she'd had a heart attack, and from that day on she went to church and never smoked. Lisa always told me "You're lucky your ma's so young," but truth is she wasted it on that heart attack. Anyhow she arranged for tests, my ma, and I set off meaning to have them, but on a billboard I saw a girl with black teeth under the words *Meth Destroys*. Something gunned in me like a jake brake and I decided to go find that girl, get her high. I went to Ray's and he walked out in his boxers followed by his wife. "You slept?" he said.

"That was a week ago."

"So you slept."

"Can I come in?"

There was this Indian in their house, and the four of us messed around while a pit bull watched from a cage. Next thing, the Indian was leading Sheila and her kids away. "I'll never see those kids again," Ray wept.

I wondered if I'd missed something. "Is there more?"

"You want to be my bitch?"

"What do you mean?"

He reached over, stuffed my balls between my legs, and said, "My bitch." We drove across to Cherokee and played slots until we had cash to start cooking again. He had me wear Sheila's panties when I went out for Sudafed. Law makes you buy just a little at each store, but it adds up. So does the money, and we were broke when AT&T offered ten thousand dollars to let them put a tower on Ray's land. They disguised it like a pine and birds nested in it like it was any other tree. Ray would come upstairs with these water bottles full of lithium and xylene and lye and say, Go for a bike ride. In my bottle cages it all sloshed around and mixed up while I climbed to Davenport Gap. Up there one day, I entered a cloud that hit me with a spray of mist and then I was opening a bottle, offering my mix to the cloud. Just then, a car sped by. I chased it down the slope and caught it, flipped it off, sped home to Ray.

"Where's the other bottle?" he said.

I seized up: I'd left it at the gap.

"You drink it?"

"Can you drink it?"

"Well, you'll die."

At first I believed I had. "Guess that's your punishment," he said.

"Don't you care if I die?"

"There's more of you where you came from."

That kind of emptied me out. "Just kidding," he said after a while.

"So you think there's more of me."

"Well, just fetch that bottle."

Folks would come at all hours. There was a deputy who bought five hundred at a time and we would listen to his cop radio. One day a dude filed a complaint that his wife had pissed in his mug of coffee. "Call and say we'll report to the scene," said Ray.

We piled in, Ray and the cop in front, me behind the grid. The siren screamed as we sped across town. At the man's house Ray told me, "Stay." I tried to get out anyhow but I was locked up. Whole hours passed before they came out, chuckling.

"What happened?" I said when they were in the car.

"Filed a report," said the cop, and then a look passed between him and Ray.

"Did he think you were both cops?" I asked as we drove off.

"Maybe you should beat him with your stick."

"Replaced our sticks with Tasers."

"Tase him, then."

"Why don't you?"

"Won't fit through the bars."

"I'll pull over."

We veered off onto a dirt path and then Ray got out. "Stand up," he barked at me. A wild boar was watching us from the woods. It had come to protect me, but Ray would tase it too. Stay back, I begged it in my head, and Ray lifted the Taser and at the last moment, as I shook, he said, "Just kidding."

Things got better. We drove to a cockfight and busted it up, then went to another and won some cash. There was a guy the cop told us was Dolly Parton's brother. He smoked with us and Ray said, "Where's your big tits," and when he got mad Ray pulled the Taser out and tased him. We took off. The cop got to talking about Dolly and her songs. He said she'd written more songs than anyone in history, thousands upon thousands of them. "I admire that," he said. "Me, I've written ten, maybe twelve songs."

I said, "I bet she'd be having fun if she was here with us."

I got scared they'd tase me again, but they laughed and the cop started singing. That was around when she got in and rode along with us for a bit. She'd done this deal with the governor called Imagination Library, where poor kids get free books. It was on some billboards we were passing, and Ray's kids had read some of those books. Why she was in the car, she'd found out Ray'd stole them from her. I thought to warn him but I looked up and the next light was for her road, Dolly Parton Parkway. The cop thought his own fingers were the ones that hit the signal, and I froze and next thing we're at Dale's, but if I tell you we watched Dale screw his girl and took his cash and pistol-whipped him, you won't see how I sat frozen while that bitch stared through me, steering us toward hell. She wanted to show me what happens in hell when you give AIDS to your wife. She had it from her husband, and that's what her songs were about. She wouldn't kill us just yet cause it would all be there waiting, come time.

I woke up alone with a note by the bed that said, "Call your mom." I drove to my ma's and let myself in to find her at her table, writing. "Knock knock," I said.

"Hi," she told me without looking up.

"You copying a recipe?"

"Where's Lisa?"

"Is it your brownies?"

"Who's Ray?"

"He's my blood brother."

I could see she wasn't meaning to bake brownies. There were some medical instruments lying around—a blood pressure cuff, a stethoscope, a roll of gauze—along with several pill bottles, like she was intending to put Ray out of business.

"Lisa called here not fifteen minutes ago."

"So then you know where she is already."

"She told me she was at Krystal."

I can't explain. It was like all women were inside her right then, cussing at me for not wanting them hard enough. I got to feeling she was a cop. I said, "If you're so naïve, why'd you have that heart attack?" I knew I just needed a hit, so I headed back to Ray's, but no one was home.

For the first time I went down to the basement and turned the knob. There he was in a chair, wearing a shirt and nothing else, waiting.

It took me a second to react. I jumped and hit my head on the low ceiling.

"Remember when you told me you'd break my arm?" he said.

I shook my head, stammering *sorry*.

"How would you do it?"

"I know you don't want me down here."

"Tell you what, go buy some whiskey. Here's twenty bucks."

I stumbled over myself running back upstairs. I knew he'd call his buddies, which was too much to bear. I sped fast through the holler. I ran over a dog and decided it belonged to a boy who told his dad my license plate, so now I'd have to go back the long way while Ray screwed the whole state.

The clerk was a lady I hadn't seen before, with icy eyes the color of blue Kool-Aid. "Back for more?" she said.

"Huh?"

"Run out?"

She was nodding at me, her curls bobbing along with her nods. "Of what?"

"George Dickel?" she said, and I thought, maybe I've got a twin, maybe Ray's doing him right now and drinking his Dickel.

"I'm an only child."

"I'm the youngest of ten."

As she stared through me, I felt more fear than any soldier at war, but she rang me up and let me go. On the way home, the long way, I passed the black-toothed billboard girl and tried to count my teeth with my tongue but I lost count. I recalled finding Lisa on the phone with her friend, giggling about me. She thought Ray was part of her plan but the joke was on her, because I was in love, and I decided then to help Ray get his kids back.

I carried the bottle in and presented it. "Look," Ray said, gesturing out the window behind me.

I turned and saw the pine woods across the road. "You mad about the basement?"

He shook his head. "While you were gone," he said, "I realized I hate you."

I figured Ray was joking, so I laughed.

"That's what a pussy you are. I say I hate you, and you laugh."

I set the whiskey down and asked what was going on.

"I got you fucked up and fucked your marriage up and never used a rubber and your ma won't talk to you, but you keep on liking me."

"So I should hate you?"

"So I should hate you?" he mimicked in the high voice of a pussy.

"What is it you want me to do?"

Ray shook his head. "Nothing. Stay here. I'm gonna go find my wife."

He walked out. "Stop," I called out, tearing up, and he pointed at my face and said, "There's the problem with you."

After that, things changed. I started wishing to lose my teeth out of plain spite. I looked around for the billboard girl and found her in Knoxville. Her name was April, and she took me to see some folks. There was a dude that hot-wired cars, who drove me to the Atlanta bathhouse. He left after a few days, but I stayed on. Your body needs dreams, but you can get them while you're awake. Every few days I bought something to eat from a machine. One day I got sick with fever chills, then I got better. When I finally went outside, two weeks had passed, because that was how long my car had been impounded. The bill was twelve hundred dollars, which meant it was totaled. I walked to Big Lots, found a truck, and hot-wired it, which was the start of not being a pussy. I got on I-75 South. The sun was rising as I reached Miami. I looked in the rearview and saw how the weeks of fasting had sculpted my face, which led me to meet some folks. We drank rum in pools and sang "Auld Lang Syne" and one day I froze up and realized it had never gotten cold.

"It don't," said Vince, the silver-haired guy I'd been hanging with, but there'd been others, too; now suddenly we were alone.

"What month is it?"

"March," he said.

"I had a birthday."

"Well, happy birthday." A grin stretched out from either side of his cigar. I asked if he'd seen my phone. "They turned it off," he said, "remember?"

I felt uneasy as he handed me his. Outside on a deck facing the canal I called the only number I could remember. It rang twice before I got an error message. If I wanted, it said, I could hang up and try again.

"City and state?" the 411 machine said.

I had to grip the railing to keep from tumbling into the water. "Pigeon Forge, Tennessee. Dr. Lighter."

They connected me automatically. Each ring was a shock to my chest but I kept holding on. "Doctor's office," my wife said.

I spoke her name and she said, "You're alive."

"Where's my ma?"

"We tried to find you."

"Lisa, come on."

"It was in November, she—"

I threw the phone in the canal. The number was on her caller ID, though. She could give it to the cops. That's what I'm most ashamed of: worrying about her caller ID when I'd just learned about my ma.

I never went back in. I walked around to the garage for my truck. Twelve hours later a sign said *Welcome to Tennessee*. Below those words it said the state was home to Vice President Al Gore. Except that had been years ago, before anything went wrong. I sort of broke down, right there on the shoulder. A cop asked what was the matter and I pointed to the sign. He said get on up the road, so that's what I did. For several more months I got on up the road to wherever I could. I figured I'd keep smoking till I died, which would happen when my mind ran out of dreams. All I had to do, I realized, was quit dreaming. I would drive through the night, and when I started dreaming, I slapped myself. One morning I rounded a curve and saw the moon over Mount Cammerer. It had never risen so late before. I decided to start keeping a list of the things it does. I wrote down a whole book of them, which could have broken some ground, but there was no use, so I ripped it up and kept driving. Some preacher on the radio who'd been shouting about patience asked, What will you miss when you're dead?

I was overtaking a car. It was the stretch where Dolly Parton Parkway loses that name and goes down to two lanes. There was a sign for Forbidden Caverns. I know how it works in those caves, you go through them together in a group. The group gets to know each other and makes friends. What will you miss, said the man, and I looked at the hills and thought, Nothing. Not Lisa, since I can't stand what I did, and not my ma because she's gone. As for Ray, my head sent a signal to my foot just as a semi rounded the bend.

I sped up, hoping to crash into it. The driver would live because his truck was so big, but if he didn't, I'd already hurt plenty of folks anyway. I wondered if my ma would be there when I died, shaking her head along with the Lord. I started to cry. My vision blurred and I figured it would keep on blurring from there into oblivion, but at the last minute the trucker ruined it by steering onto the dirt.

That's when I drove back up the Pigeon River gorge to the I-40 rest area. Once again I sat there touching myself as families pulled in and their dogs peed and finally a Hummer parked beside me. "You party?" said a fellow in a Braves cap.

His windows had a full tint, so we put down the seats and messed around, nothing special till he pulled a phone out and said, "Know about this?"

"About your phone?"

He swiped the screen and I looked down to see a grid of

thumbnail pictures labeled with names. "It's in order of how close they are."

I touched one, and the screen filled up with a guy named Josh. *10 Miles Away*, it said in the corner. "So it knows where I am?"

"No, it knows where *I* am."

"Moon's about to rise."

I pointed through the sickly tint of the Braves fan's rear window. Ten seconds later it began to peek above the mountain.

"Here's a dude looking. See the green dot?"

I took the phone and stared down at Ray, at his inimitable fish eyes.

To appear calm, I stopped breathing. Ray's skin was pale as ever. I guessed he hadn't found his wife.

"Hit 'chat,'" the guy said.

It occurred to me to type, "hey," which floated up the screen in a yellow bubble. Seconds later came the response: "Sup?"

"Say 'looking.'"

"Not much," I wrote instead, and then "Horned up" chirped onscreen.

The guy grabbed the phone from me and typed with both hands. I watched the moon rise and shrink while my gut did the opposite. "Dude says come over," he exclaimed.

I had always thought people were idiots when they talked about natural highs, but I'd just never gotten jealous enough to feel one until then. "I'll tail you," I said. He was too fucked up to notice me pocket his phone. I followed him as far as the Newport exit, where I fell back. As soon as he'd passed it, I got off. I figured I had till morning before the account froze. Several miles from Ray's house, I pulled into Hardee's. Five guys had green dots: Clay, James, Anchovi, Just Lookin, and Kid.

Kid was Ray, twelve miles off. I checked my own profile: I wasn't the Hummer fellow, but a mixed-race guy called Tyrone, twenty-one, headline reading, "Don't fall in love with everyone you see."

I ordered a hamburger. A journey faced me with infinite directions that led out twelve miles apiece. To confront Ray, I had to try each one, on roads that twisted in on themselves so many times— but suddenly Kid was ten miles off.

I hit the button again and it said nine. He was coming home.

I thought of that AT&T phone tower, disguised as a jack pine, and how readily Ray had agreed to it. He must have already been Kid, even back then.

When they handed me my burger, I thought I might puke, but something in me reached out and devoured it and it revved me up with gas for the first time in days. I channeled that power into the engine and took off toward Ray's. It felt good not being a pussy. Five miles, said the phone. The radio preacher was saying we're made of dust and it won't take much air for the Lord to blow us away. One lung of the Lord, said the preacher, is bigger than the world. I pulled up to Ray's. The phone said seven again, as if he'd rigged up some decoy. I had one too: I looked like Tyrone, unless Ray had put a green dot in my head.

That's how it will be in a few more years, I was thinking as I felt my way to the basement: we'll drive all night looking for folks, but in our head.

I plugged in the bulb. It swung on a cord in front of a mirror reflecting a St. Andrew's cross and a workhorse. I walked to the closet and swung the plank, and there was the bowie knife, its handle wood and its blade curved and I'd forgotten what war it came from.

I was climbing the stairs again when my phone rang.

"Where are you?" said somebody called Damien Warman. "You two think you can treat me like this?"

I decided to practice not being a pussy. "Where are you?"

"Oh, come on, screw you."

"No, I asked you a question. If you want to live—if you want to survive another minute of your worthless life, answer it."

There was a gulp. "Where's Tyrone?"

"Dead. You're next."

"Where is he?"

"No, tell me where you are."

"Downtown Hilton."

"Well, you best get yourself out of that downtown Hilton."

What a thrill it gave me, saying those things. I hung up, and then the screen showed the earth in space, the clouds moving in real time. Mountains inching toward dawn. I guess the camera was on the moon. In anticipation of sunrise, my blood heated up. Just as I was about to catch fire, Damien Warman's name flashed across outer space again. To be a pussy was to answer, "Just kidding," so I hit "ignore," found a jug of bourbon, took a swig, and realized the dog should be barking.

I went upstairs to his cage, in which he lay dead. That bothered me. "Sup?" said a new message from Kid, four miles away.

I went out into the night and ran the knife blade along my finger. "Not much," I wrote, bleeding as I typed. It felt strange, so I pricked another finger, rubbed the blood on my pants.

The cuts stung. I'd gotten so sober that I could feel pain.

As time slowed, I looked up at the moon bisected by the pine. If it was broadcasting my thoughts to Ray, I didn't care; I was ready for him. I checked the distance. Two miles away: curvy miles, so I figured I had about four minutes.

I typed, "Zeela Tipton 1950–2009," and read about my ma's journey to meet the Lord. She was survived by two brothers and a daughter-in-law, said the obituary, and no one else. There wasn't time to fret about that. I might be meeting the Lord soon myself, and I wanted to show him there was some good in me, so I typed Lisa's number in and wrote to Lisa, "Ask Dr. Lighter for a blood test."

The noise of a motor faded and grew closer. The phone said 800 feet. I went in and turned off the lights. A siren blared for a split second and quit. Through the peephole I watched a single shadow climb out. It lurched forward and grew larger. I had read the obituary to help urge myself ahead. She has traveled to meet the Lord, I said to myself, moving from the hinged to the unhinged side of the door.

Last thing before it swung open, I looked at the phone, which said zero feet.

His hand reached through the dark. I clutched the knife and plunged it into his arm. It sank into his flesh. I pulled it out and saw his eyes bulge as I stabbed again. He lunged toward me, spurting blood. I held tight onto the hilt. "Sandra," he said as he sank, which is when I knew what that siren had meant.

He contorted away, making gurgly noises. I let go and ran out. The cruiser window was open, and I could hear cops on the radio. "How do you know a Kentucky girl's on the rag?" one of the cops asked, and then they all laughed as the pines heard my own phone ring.

Me, I've written ten, maybe twelve songs.

"Babe?" said Ray when I answered. "I heard you're back in town."

"How'd you hear that," I managed to say.

"I was on my way to you, but I drove into the river."

"I don't live at your house anymore."

"Lisa never answers your door."

"I gave her AIDS. I caught it from you."

"But you never came down with the flu."

"You ruined my life, Ray."

"I have some crystal."

The blue of the light bar gleamed in moonlight as Ray told me he was at the S-curve. "I was scared of how much I liked you," he said.

"That's retarded," I said.

"But I'm trying to say things I mean."

The front door wouldn't budge. I broke the window with a brick, climbed in, and saw the cop sitting up against the door, meeting the Lord. I reached in his pants for Ray's phone. I checked the distance against Tyrone's: 2000 feet. A chill went through me to think Ray had been talking from the cop's pocket. If I was high, I might have tried to saw down the cell tower, but he was at the S-curve.

I knew that.

I put the phone in my pants with the other two, where they could all signal each other if they wanted. Driving the cruiser, I took Ray's out to check the messages. *Sup. Hey stud. Where u at.* One was named Lucifer and he was ten miles away. I imagined him ten miles down into the earth. I passed Dollywood, which is on a back road in a holler, not where you'd expect. Deeper into the forest I pulled off by a precipice. At the bottom of a ravine Ray stood by his wrecked car in water to his knees.

I left two of the phones on the seat, got the knife, and scooted downhill to the bank. "That's my knife," he said from across the water.

"I'll slit your throat with it," I told him, brushing dirt off.

He opened his mouth, then shut it. "The crystal got wet."

"I'm not afraid of you anymore."

"Then get on with it." He pointed to his neck.

"That's the oldest trick in the book."

"Mark's on his way. Cop from the dogfight."

"I doubt we'll be seeing Mark."

"I made a deal with him. He'll file it as a suicide."

"Why don't you piss off, Ray."

"No, it's really what he's coming here for."

Ray's eyes were fixed on mine, but it was easy to look Ray in the eye and still hate him. Nor was I touched by the sound of his voice. I hadn't been prepared, though, for the effect of his breath when I waded into the river. It smelled of bourbon and smoke and instantly I was back in Lubbock drinking bourbon with him, holding him in the bed, thinking he was only a lonely child.

"It's for my kids," he said. "If you had kids, you'd understand."

I stepped onto a bar of gravel and kicked some into the water. I guessed there was a fair chance he was telling the truth.

"I've been down in Florida," I said.

"I like it there. Took Angel and Ray Junior to the Daytona 500. Remember at the Bristol Speedway, when you thought we were dying?"

I shook my head. "I've never been to Bristol."

"You were pretty lit up then."

"You were as lit up as me."

"But I was aware of it. You, you acted surprised."

With no memory of Bristol I tried to imagine that city, which straddles Virginia and Tennessee. I pictured a dotted state line painted down the middle of downtown. I did remember a line like that, but it had been in Mexico. Fast cars racing in circles, steered by remote. They crashed over and over until the stadium was about to explode. Panicked, I dragged Ray out into a country I'd never seen. What happened next, Ray punched me, right in front of all the Mexicans. "Now you'll have a black eye for your ma's birthday," he said. He still drove me to her house but by then we were in Leo, and Ma was a Cancer. I staggered in and found her on the couch with her quilting circle—three ladies who together weighed less than me, sitting in a row like sticks of brittle.

"This is my son," said my mother.

I can't account for what came next. I looked down at the quilt, a patchwork maze whose path mapped all that I'd done wrong in her eyes. I saw my house when the bank forced Lisa out of it. I saw her in the future, dying of AIDS. I saw Ma getting sick and writing in my baby book: a list of my firsts, which she was coding into the quilt as triangles arranged in a loop. With that loop she was telling me I would never change. "Up yours with a plunger if that's what you think," I said, which Ma must have taken as a response to her words.

I stepped into the icy water and sat on Ray's car hood. I knew he wouldn't change. "I need you alive," I told him, taking his hand.

He slipped on the algae but I held on, pulling him toward me. "You were about to kill me," he said.

"I don't have anyone else."

"You've got Lisa."

"I don't want her."

"You want me?"

"You're better than nothing."

He put his hands in his pockets and kicked at some rocks. "That came out wrong," I said, and he looked at the shore and said, "No, it's true."

The phone purred in my pants. Ray took it out and squinted. It was Tyrone's.

"This guy says he's glad I'm online again," he said.

"I wonder what that could mean."

Ray pressed his fingertips to the holes in mine. "Can you

drive?" he said, glancing at his smashed car. The river was roaring around it, rising toward its broken window. He squeezed my hand. High tide must be on the way, and if mountain rivers had tides, then tides were everywhere. Those lithium-and-lye bottles had tides. Flasks had them; so did tree sap, gas tanks, storm drains, even the blood in my heart. I squeezed back. "So long as we find a dry bag of crystal," I said, because—here's how sober I was—I could feel high tide in my veins, surging toward the moon, cresting like it must have done every day of my life.

ACKNOWLEDGMENTS

I would like to thank the following organizations for their support in recent years while I've worked on this and other projects: Caldera Arts Center, The Camargo Foundation, The Robert M. MacNamara Foundation, The Virginia Center for the Creative Arts, Fundación Valparaíso, The Corporation of Yaddo, The Brown Foundation Fellows Program at the Dora Maar House, The Ucross Foundation, The Millay Colony for the Arts, The Djerassi Resident Artists Program, and The Creative Capital Foundation. I'm also grateful for the help and support of Jason Cook at Fiddleblack, everyone at Sarabande—especially Sarah Gorham, Kirby Gann, and Kristen Radtke—and my agent, Samantha Shea.

JOHN MCMANUS is the author of the novel *Bitter Milk* and the short story collections *Born on a Train* and *Stop Breakin Down*. His work has appeared in *Ploughshares, Tin House, McSweeney's, American Short Fiction, Oxford American,* and elsewhere. He is the recipient of the Whiting Writers' Award, the Fellowship of Southern Writers' New Writing Award, and a Creative Capital Literature grant. He lives in Virginia.

Sarabande Books is a nonprofit literary press located in Louisville, KY, and Brooklyn, NY. Founded in 1994 to champion poetry, short fiction, and essay, we are committed to creating lasting editions that honor exceptional writing. For more information, please visit sarabandebooks.org.